MARIE-HÉLÈNE LEBEAULT

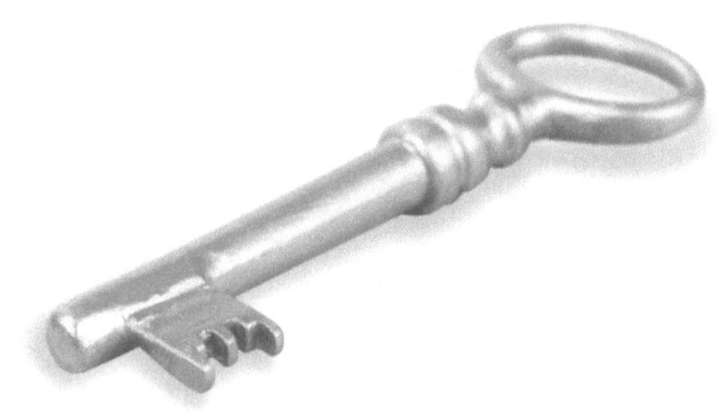

THE ANCESTORS' KEY

THE EVERS SERIES BOOK ONE

First published by Beaches and Trails Publishing 2020

2025 Edition
Editing by Jacki Corn-Uys
Cover by Getfast

DEDICATION

For my two adorable teenagers.
We're finally the same age.

ACKNOWLEDGMENT

Many thanks to my good friend Denise Drolet for reading the terrible second draft and providing tons of excellent comments and suggestions.

CHAPTER 1
LEAVING

"IT'S JUST NOT FAIR! It's our senior year!" wailed Lola as she fell face-first onto the bed.

Jane, her best friend, giggled at her dramatics but sobered up, remembering this was a dire situation indeed. "Why can't you just move in with me and my mom?" asked Jane, plopping down on the bed next to Lola.

Lola's turned her head to respond so Jane could hear her. "The law says I have to live with a blood relative if I have one. And if I didn't, I'd be put into a foster home......" Lola's voice trailed off as the severity of the situation started to sink in. It was too much to bear, so she put her pillow over her head.

Jane grinned. Lola was such a goofball! She took the pillow off Lola's head and tugged at her arm so she would sit up, and they could talk like ordinary people. "But it's not like you're a kid. You'll be sixteen over the summer. I know people who leave home at that age!" exclaimed Jane. "My cousin Sherry moved in with her boyfriend when she was just fourteen! Of course, she was trying to get away from Aunt Myra's lecherous new boyfriend, but still. Gavin was only sixteen. He quit school and got a job, she stayed in school, and it all worked out in the end!"

Lola sat up and gave her friend a hopeless look. "Right, but they have jobs, money, a car......I have none of those things."

Jane got up and started pacing back and forth on the purple shag carpet that had seen better days. She had that concentrated look she got when she's problem-solving or hatching a plan. She was tapping just above her lip, and after a while, she asked, "But what about your inheritance? Surely, you'll get something?"

"Yes, of course. The first bit when I'm eighteen, then another when I'm twenty-one, and the final one when I'm thirty-five!" Lola cried out in response.

"Thirty-five! You'll be ancient!" exclaimed Jane. She went over to her friend and gave her a big hug, then rested her head on her shoulder. "That sucks! I'll miss you so much. Promise you'll text me every day," pleaded Jane.

"I will, but I'm not sure what will happen to my cell phone. All our accounts are being closed......" added Lola as she shrugged, unsure as to whether or not she was indeed heading into the unknown, alone.

"Well, you'll get another, and you'll send me your new number," said Jane, trying to be chipper. "Or you'll call, send an email, send an owl for God's sake! Just make sure you keep in touch!" screeched Jane. The panic in Jane's eyes made Lola realize how worried she was about her predicament.

"You don't have to worry; I'd die without you. Of course, I'll find a way." She kissed Jane's cheek and stroked her back soothingly.

Jane relaxed and got practical. "How long will the bus ride take, anyway?" she inquired, hoping there was a way they might still see each other regularly.

"It's four hours from Baltimore to Williamsburg and about fifteen minutes to the house after that," replied Lola.

"Bummer. It's not like we can see each other every weekend," Jane whined.

"Right, but maybe we can visit when there's a long weekend or something, and of course over the summer," said Lola, perking up.

Jane looked unsure. "Sure, that'll work. But you know, I'll be getting a job this summer to save for college. I guess I'll let you know when I get my schedule. So, when do you leave exactly?"

Lola got up to look at her planner. "Final exams are on Thursday, June 20th. I'll be on the 10 a.m. bus on the following Sunday. The new owners want the house ASAP to start their renovations," replied Lola, turning back to Jane.

"Why doesn't your aunt come to get you? Won't you have a ton of stuff?" asked Jane.

"She doesn't drive for some reason," replied Lola, shrugging her shoulders. Jane waited for further details, but Lola just stood there.

"What, is she mentally disabled? In a wheelchair? Too old to drive? What's her name, anyway?" quizzed Jane, unwilling to let it go.

"Her name is Phyllis. I think my mom said she has epilepsy. She's not old; she's only forty-five. And I'm pretty sure she knows how to drive, but I think her medication makes her sleepy or something," Lola responded.

"Oh, that sucks. But then who's going to pick you up you from the bus terminal? You don't have to walk, do you? Because that would be beyond lame!"

Lola only had a few details to share, but at least this was taken care of. "Her neighbor, Jackson," said Lola.

"Right. Do you need help packing?" asked Jane.

"Nah, I'm not bringing much. The executors sold off almost everything of value to pay off our debts. Simone, my mom's best friend, will pack up the stuff that goes to goodwill. I'm just taking my clothes, my iPad, and a few mementos. It all fits in a backpack and this Rubbermaid bin. My aunt will have a room set up for me when I get there," explained Lola.

Jane peered into the bin and exclaimed, "You travel light!" She grabbed Lola's favorite book. "So, what's she like, your aunt?"

Lola thought for a moment. "I don't really remember my aunt. After my dad left, we didn't see much of his side of the family, and with the distance, we sort of lost touch," she mused.

"It's too bad your dad died too; you could have gone to live with him," said Jane.

"I don't think so. From what my mom said, he was always a bit of a flake and could barely take care of himself. That's why he eventually moved back with his sister. And they both lived in their parents' house, the house I'm about to move into," Lola stated.

"They are either dirt poor or super-rich. They must be rich! Only rich people live in their houses with their adult family members. Maybe that's how they get rich! If you never have to pay for housing, heating, electricity, the savings must add up! Is it a big house?" asked Jane.

"Yeah, I think it is," Lola replied. "It's a traditional Victorian House, according to the lawyer. I've never been there. But here, he gave me a picture. Look!"

Jane took the picture from Lola's hand and peered at it. Her eyes widened instantly. "Creepy!"

Lola laughed, took the picture back, and replied, "Only because it's a black and white picture. It's actually pink if you can believe it! But I know what you mean. That is exactly how I felt when I first saw it."

She stared down at the picture again. At least four stories high, the house was huge, with a tall main section that looked just like a tower and two wings with turrets on each side. One side had a huge covered porch with ivy overhangs for privacy. Lola pointed at the porch. "They must use this area a lot—it seems to have more furniture in it than my entire house!" The other wing was similar but had floor-to-ceiling windows and resembled a sunroom. The lawyer called it a Conservatory. The front door was flanked by expansive, frosted windows and had its own imposing porch and broad steps that led to a long walkway, met by a fountain of all things.

"Straight out of a Jane Austen novel!" exclaimed Jane.

Three other paths seemed to lead away from the fountain. "I wonder where these other paths lead to?" mused Lola.

Jane peered at the picture, then looked off into space, obviously trying to imagine it. "Maybe they'll have a pool and a tennis court? Maybe one of them leads to a garage? We don't see one on the picture, but surely, they have one?"

Lola nodded and said, "Well, I guess I'll find out soon enough."

CHAPTER 2

JOURNEY

THE SUNDAY BUS left at 10 a.m. as scheduled. An ungodly hour for teenagers, which meant that Lola slept most of the way.

Besides being tired from the early hour, she was exhausted from the last couple of weeks. She'd been allowed to stay in her house until her finals were over, and she was grateful for it. She had her routine, and, despite missing her mom like crazy, it just felt better to be home. Simone, her mom's best friend, came to live with her and help pack up the house to focus on her studies and her grief. Lola had always liked Simone. She was funny, spontaneous, and quirky. Everything her mom wasn't. Simone claimed her mom hadn't always been such a stick-in-the-mud that apparently, she was quite the hellion in their youth! Lola only saw her mom as the caring, responsible adult she became after her dad left. Simone said her mom was sick of shenanigans, empty dreams, and broken promises.

Lola's mom had worked as a dental assistant at a clinic in Waverly, Baltimore. She walked to work every day and always seemed to enjoy it because Lola never heard her complain. It was a decent enough paying job but never seemed to be sufficient to pay off their debts. Lola didn't think there would be any money left when she turned eighteen unless her mom had been secretly putting money aside all these years. And since both her grandparents were dead, and her mom had no siblings, Lola was on her own.

She and her mom got along. They never fought, but they were never really close, like Jane and her mom. Those two were like BFFs. Having long talks about boys, swapping clothes, even just the two of them going on road trips. Jane claimed her mom needed those moments more than she did to get away from the boys—the boys being Jane's three younger brothers aged eleven, nine, and seven. But Lola could see they were a close-knit family. She'd always envied their easy camaraderie at mealtimes. Everybody listened to the happenings in each other's days and still had words of encouragement when someone suffered a bad one. The boys didn't seem to be constantly fighting like most brothers did, though they were a lively bunch. Lola would have loved a family like this one! But again, she liked her privacy, her quiet moments, the calm serenity that her mother seemed to cultivate in their home. It certainly helped make Lola more self-sufficient, which would prove essential in her new life.

Simone told her that her aunt Phyllis was a bit of a recluse, and it would be just the two of them in that big old house. That didn't faze Lola much. She preferred being left to her own devices than being fretted about and always watched as Simone was doing to her. Lola knew she meant well since she didn't have any kids of her own, and she was sure Simone was trying to imagine what it would feel like to lose your only remaining parent at fifteen and a mom at that.

But the truth was, even when her mom was alive, it never seemed *real*. Sure, she was a good mom. She made healthy meals, ensured Lola was cared for, well adjusted, slept enough, and had everything she truly needed, including a sympathetic ear. But she was never really there. Like she was always ticking off items from a list in her mind and alternating between lists. Good parent checklist, useful neighbor checklist, good employee checklist, good human checklist. Not a robot, but not someone with depth. At least none that she shared with Lola. Maybe she shared it with Simone......she certainly didn't share it with a boyfriend unless she snuck off at night after Lola was in bed. Dating didn't seem to be on her list of priorities. Lola always figured she wasn't over the trauma of her marriage to her dad.

Then again, Lola didn't have much of a social life herself. Other than Jane, Lola didn't have that many friends, and none of the boys, or girls, at school or in the neighborhood had ever sparked her romantic interest. She never felt like she fit in anywhere. She wasn't into sports, fashion, or even technology. Lola liked to read. Anywhere, anytime. She also fancied herself a fair enough writer but had yet to take the plunge and write an actual novel or short story like her Lit teacher kept after her to do. Longer texts seemed so daunting, as if they would take forever to write. Lola always promised herself that it would happen one day...

It wasn't like Lola was ugly or anything. Her mom had always said she was beautiful, but moms have to say that. Simone told her she was beautiful and should be dating by now like it was a rite of passage. Maybe she was a late bloomer? Or maybe she was waiting for fate to intervene? Her looks were adequate as far as she was concerned. She had nice curly brown hair that she could straighten should she ever feel moved to use a hairbrush. Her figure was okay, though leaning a bit towards curvy and voluptuous, which got her looks from many jocks. Even with her loose shirts, she couldn't entirely hide an impressive pair of boots, a tiny waist, and wide, full hips. Her legs were on the short side, but she thought her height was respectable at 5'6". Not so short as to be called a shrimp and not so tall that she intimidated any of the guys. Call her old-fashioned, but she wanted him to be taller than her when she did get a boyfriend.

Lola really liked her eyes. They were technically dark blue, but they often seemed violet when the light was right or if she was angry or had been crying. It made her feel unique. There was only one feature that Lola was less than content with—her teeth. They were crooked, both top and bottom. And she had that one top tooth that stuck out when she smiled, that made her tend to smile with her mouth closed. Her mom said it was endearing. To Lola, it was just an ad for the braces she couldn't afford. Even with her mom's employee discount, there was no way they could fit it in the budget. And now, well, she'd have to learn to live with it. Crooked teeth were the least of her worries.

CHAPTER 3
ARRIVING

SHE WOKE with a start as someone placed a hand on her shoulder. "This is your stop," said the older lady in the seat next to her. "You're Lola, right? The bus driver called out your name." Lola mumbled her thanks, grabbed her backpack, and headed for the door. The driver had already removed her bin from the bus, and soon she was left alone with all her worldly belongings at the ATM Express waiting for the infamous Jackson.

Luckily, the wait was short. She barely had time to sit on her bin when an old, beat-up, blue pickup truck arrived, spluttering fumes, and heaving to a stop as though it had just died. *I bet you that Jackson is as ancient as his truck*, Lola thought to herself. But to Lola's utter amazement, a tall, lanky, not-ancient boy stepped out of the cab and scowled at her.

"Where's the rest of your stuff?" he said.

Lola stared blankly up at the boy. Speech seemed to evade her as she took in the most unusual shade of green eyes she'd ever seen. They weren't an emerald green or a brownish-green, more like the color of a Jade stone with a slight turquoise tint to it. The color was so striking because the boy was otherwise completely dressed in black. Normally that would make a person look drab and ordinary, but there was something otherworldly about him. Lola rubbed her eyes, thinking she might still be a little groggy from sleeping on the bus. Maybe it was just the contrast with their surroundings, but to Lola, he looked like he'd just walked out of one of her favorite comic books. The dark ones, with limited color. They are mostly black and white, but where only hues of blue and green are colored in, they pop off the page in their starkness. This is how the boy appeared to Lola, with crisp lines and sharp colors.

"Phyllis didn't say her relation was slow......" and with that, he rolled his eyes. He had a slight southern accent and spoke in the slow, leisurely way they seem to have in the south. It somehow didn't suit his sleek, all-black appearance.

Lola snapped out of her daze and scowled back at him. "I'm not slow. I was expecting an old geezer named Jackson!"

"*I'm* Jackson. My friends call me Jack, but you can call me Jackson. Come on. I don't have all day," he snapped.

Great! Lola thought. *This is going to be a fun ride. Fifteen minutes of gas fumes, shaking truck, and a sour boy.* Lola grabbed her backpack and let Jackson deal with the bin. She waited for him to open the door, but he just hopped in on his side and barked, "Get in!" *So much for southern manners!*

He managed to start the truck up and eased onto the road without incident. Lola clutched her backpack to herself and kept her eyes on the road. There wasn't much scenery to look at near the highway, but as they drove deeper into the country and onto small roads, trees and flowers started popping up. It was a lovely day in late June. Not too hot, not too humid. Jackson must have appreciated her restraint because he chose this exact moment to end the silence between them.

"So, when was the last time you visited your aunt?" he asked.

"Apparently, my family and I stayed there for a week when I was about two years old while my grandmother was still alive. I assume my aunt was there, but I obviously don't remember," Lola replied.

"Miss Evers is the most gracious person I know. She's a good baker too," he added wistfully. *Interesting description indeed.*

Lola thought about her next question carefully and then asked,

"My aunt said you were her neighbor. You don't look old enough to be a homeowner, so I guess your parents are the neighbors?"

"No, I live on the Evers property, in an apartment over the garage," Jackson replied easily.

"How did that happen?" Lola said quizzically.

"Well, my grandpa used to be Mrs. Evers' groundskeeper, and my grandma was the housekeeper. They lived in a cottage on the property. My dad was born there, and when they passed away, he came back and took over for them with my mom," Jackson explained.

"So, your parents now work for my aunt?"

"No," Jackson corrected her. "A few years ago, there was a fire in the woods near our cottage, and the flames could not be contained. My parents never had a chance," he said flatly like he'd told the story so many times, it didn't faze him anymore.

"Oh. My. God! I'm so sorry! How did you survive?" Lola's eyes were wide with shock.

"I was away at school......" Jackson's voice trailed off as he stared at the road ahead.

"I'm really sorry. I guess we have more in common than I realized. My parents are dead too," said Lola mournfully.

"I know," Jackson replied. "Phyllis told me about your mom. And, well, I was here when your dad died, though I don't remember much. I must have been six years old."

"Right. How old are you now?" Lola inquired.

"I just turned nineteen. You?"

"I'm fifteen, but my birthday is in a week."

"Oh, okay. You still have a year of high school to do."

"Yeah, what's the school like?"

"I wouldn't know. I went away to school in Woodbury. Phyllis was nice enough to take over the payments when my parents died so I could finish high school and get into a good college. But my heart wasn't in it, and I came back after I graduated. I've been working for Miss Evers ever since."

"But don't you want to go to college and get a real job?" Lola queried.

"This is a real job," Jackson replied through gritted teeth.

"I mean, you know, one where you can put your mind to work," Lola answered quickly.

"My mind gets plenty of work with Phyllis. She's got me doing the books as well as taking care of the property. I do just about everything except cooking, cleaning, and laundry. She has a lady come in to do those chores a couple of times a week," said Jackson, visibly annoyed.

"So, no more housekeeper?" asked Lola.

"Nah, Phyllis says she likes her privacy, and she just couldn't get used to someone other than my mom 'lurking about,' as she calls it," he said with a smile.

"Is it true my aunt is epileptic, and that's why she can't drive?"

"That's right. She takes medication to control it," Jackson explained. "It's one of the reasons I came back. I didn't particularly appreciate knowing she was all alone in that big old house. It's good you're here, now," he added.

They fell silent again for a while, and then Lola saw it. She didn't remember a private lane bordered by tall trees. It was straight off of a movie set! And of course, there was her aunt, waiting on the steps in a long flowing dress with a light flowery print. At least, Lola figured it was her aunt. Jackson brought the car around the fountain and right to the steps, with such amazing timing that as she got to the last step, Miss Evers just had to open the door and let Lola out.

"Let me look at you!" she cried.

"Um, hi," Lola said, a blush creeping up her face.

"Don't be shy, Lola. We're going to be great friends," her aunt stated emphatically.

While they were cautiously eyeing each other, Jackson dropped off her stuff and, as discreetly as possible with such a noisy truck, drove back to the garage, and they didn't see him for the rest of the afternoon.

CHAPTER 4
MEETING

"COME ALONG, dear. You must be famished!" cooed her aunt in a thick southern drawl.

"Well, actually, I packed a lunch and ate it on the bus," Lola said lamely.

"Nonsense! I can see you need fattening up, and I'm just the woman to do it!" exclaimed Phyllis, waving away any further arguments.

She ushered Lola towards the house, daintily grabbing her backpack and depositing it by the stairs in the foyer. Then she motioned for Lola to follow her into the kitchen.

"I'll make you a nice snack, fix you a glass of iced tea, and we'll have ourselves a little chat on the porch. Then, I'll show you to your room, and you can get cleaned up or have a rest, or just get settled in."

"Um, okay, I guess." Lola was overwhelmed with her aunt's familiarity.

"Not much of a talker, are you? I guess after everything you've been through, I'd be a little shell-shocked too. You go on through that door and pick a seat on the porch—that's half the fun!" said Phyllis cheerily.

She pointed to the kitchen's right, which led into a huge dining room with at least sixteen chairs around a massive oak table. *This is gorgeous*! Thought Lola. And it certainly doesn't seem to be as stuffy as one would expect from the house's age. Lola didn't linger in the dining room, afraid that she was not meant to be there, and quickly proceeded to the large patio doors at the end of the room.

As she stepped out, she was hit by the most wonderful smell. She couldn't place it immediately, but it seemed to be coming from the numerous hanging flower pots. She'd have to ask her aunt about it. So far, she'd barely been able to string a coherent sentence together. *My aunt must think I'm an absolute simpleton!* Just then, Lola remembered her manners, and she stood up to stick her head in the door and ask if her aunt needed a hand. Her aunt, however, was already on her way with a tray full of goodies, and Lola could only stand aside and hold the door as she glided by with the practiced grace of a natural-born hostess.

Phyllis is quite pretty and doesn't look a day over 40. She looks younger than mom did, reflected Lola. Maybe it's because she didn't have to work for a living.

Phyllis arranged the tray on a side table. She poured out two tall glasses of iced tea and was holding up the sugar when she asked, "Do you take sugar in your tea?"

Lola blinked, lost in thought, and quickly replied, "Um, yes, please." Lola was still struggling to string more than a few words together.

"Go ahead, dig in. I didn't know if you were one of those vegetarians or if you had food allergies, so I brought a little of everything."

"I'm not a vegetarian, and I don't have food allergies," Lola assured her. "This looks amazing, thanks. I guess I was hungrier than I thought."

Lola loaded a plate with crustless sandwiches, grapes, cheese, and cookies. Everything looked homemade, straight out of a Martha Stewart magazine. Her aunt snagged a grape or two and drank her tea, peering at Lola. Lola could tell she was itching to ask about a thousand questions.

"I don't want to pry, dear, but are you alright? I mean generally. Everybody grieves differently, and I believe we should let people get through it in the way that works best for them if there is anything I can do. If you need to talk to someone, a counselor or me, just let me know," she stated soothingly.

"Yeah, I'm okay. I do have a question, though," Lola asked hesitantly.

"Anything, ask away!" her aunt replied.

"This might sound stupid, but what should I call you?"

"Oh, right! That's not stupid at all. You should call me Phyllis!"

"Okay, thanks, Phyllis," Lola said, happy to not have to refer to her by some strange family name.

"Anything else?"

"Where should I start looking for a job?" Lola ventured. "I turn sixteen next week."

"Oh, how exciting!" Phyllis exclaimed. "Well, you need to know that I have plenty of money to pay for your school, clothing, and any other expenses you might have. If you want a job to meet people your age, you can always ask Jackson if he has any pointers. But I think the Food Lion might be your best bet. Jackson can give you a ride into town."

"Is it very far? Can I walk? If I get a job, then I can't ask him to drive me there all the time."

"You could bike there rather easily; it would be faster. Or you could look into getting your license, and we might get you a car when school starts. I'm pretty sure taking the bus in your Senior year is unpopular."

Lola quickly interjected, "Oh, that's too much. I could buy my own car if I work all summer."

"I like your spunk, and we can argue about it later. Now, if you've finished eating, I'll take you to your room and let you settle in. We'll save the grand tour for later. Dinner is at 6 p.m., and no jeans on a Sunday," Phyllis said with a smile.

They walked back through the dining room and kitchen to the large foyer and up the stairs' curved flight. Lola could imagine ladies with sweeping gowns swaying up and down these stairs, going to balls and receiving callers. The walls were lined with portraits of who were either past occupants or perhaps ancestors.

"How old is this house?" asked Lola, intrigued.

"It was one of the first houses built in town," Phyllis answered. "It took two years to complete it, and my, or rather our, ancestors moved in in 1640. We've been here ever since."

"You mean all these people are my relatives?" Lola said, gobsmacked.

"Yes, there has always been an Evers in residence. It's a tradition. When I pass, this house will be yours, Lola."

"But surely there is someone else it should go to?" asked Lola faintly.

"I had no children, and your father was my only sibling," stated Phyllis.

"What would have happened if my dad hadn't had me?" Lola asked curiously.

"I have no idea; it's never happened. There has always been an Evers. Even before this house, our family tree goes very far back. I'll show you someday if you're interested," replied Phyllis.

"But I'm not ready to have kids! I don't even know if I want any kids!" A shudder passed through her body as she said this.

"Don't worry about that now, silly. I'm not going anywhere anytime soon! I expect to live a long, satisfying life. You won't be rid of me for quite a while!" said Phyllis cheerily.

"Oh, I didn't mean," Lola stuttered. "Um. I don't want you to die or anything. I just got here, and you're the only family I've got......" trailed Lola with a pained expression.

Phyllis must have heard the strain and barely held in tears in Lola's voice and turned to face her. Lola's body was tense, and she was giving off a vibe that said, don't touch me. Phyllis placed a hand on her shoulder and said, "You're the only family I've got. I'm so delighted you're here." Lola placed her hand on top of her aunt's and nodded her head as one of the tears slipped down her cheek. Phyllis took her hand in hers, and they walked wordlessly to Lola's room.

When the door opened, Lola realized this was the Tower Room in the picture and was immediately filled with a feeling akin to glee, which she could not explain. There wasn't a frivolous bone in her body, but this room was to die for! It wasn't overly girly, but it was feminine. Upon entering, there was what must be called a sitting room: a large three-seater sofa flanked by wooden end tables, two armchairs artfully placed to face each other, and a low, matching coffee table. Everything was perfectly symmetrical, and everything was in shades of pale gray and lilac. If Lola had friends, this would be a great place to hang out!

Behind the sofa, a few feet away, was a massive fireplace. Lola went closer to look at it and realized she could see into the bedroom. It was two-sided! On the same wall were two doors leading to the bedroom and one leading to the en-suite bathroom. The bedroom's decor was similar to the sitting room. The king-sized, four-poster bed had been stained a pale gray to match all the other wooden pieces in the room—like the bedside tables, the two trunks at the foot of the bed, and the small table between the two Queen Anne armchairs facing this side of the fireplace. Lola was starry-eyed. She trailed her fingers along with everything as they roamed about the room. Phyllis was explaining things about the room and the decor, but Lola wasn't really paying attention.

Across from the fireplace was the tower, which had been fitted with a comfy window seat for reading or lounging. Circular, wrought iron stairs led to a second-floor alcove that had been outfitted with a work desk, bookshelves, and modern technologies such as a computer, printer-scanner-fax-copy machine, and an impressive five device charging station. It was a writer's dream! At the sight of the work area, Lola couldn't suppress herself and did a little happy dance. She couldn't believe what she was seeing. *It's like someone read my mind and made this just for me*, she thought. From below, she heard her aunt ask nervously, "Do you like it?" Lola peered over the banister at her aunt and responded with a huge grin on her face. "Do I like it? Are you serious? I love it! I may never leave this alcove!"

Phyllis smiled approvingly and yelled back, "I'll leave you to it then, and see you at dinner. I hope it's not too presumptuous of me, but I've bought you a few items of clothing and had put them in your wardrobe. It's just off the en-suite bathroom. I consulted your mother's friend Simone, but if they don't fit or don't suit you, we'll return them, don't worry. It's just that I've never had anyone to shop for, and I may have gone a little crazy......" And with that, she strolled out the door. Lola counted to ten and flew down the stairs and through the entrance to the bathroom. She skidded to a stop when she realized she was in a huge walk-in closet the size of her room back home. There she found her Rubbermaid bin and her backpack on a chaise. A chaise! Cue the grapes and bonbons!

Lola looked at the racks and saw more than a few clothing items. It was a full-on wardrobe. The items were much dressier than what she normally wore, but the colors suited her complexion, and they were all the right size. As she eyed the pieces, her gaze was drawn to an outfit that looked perfect for Sunday dinner. From her aunt's appearance, the 'no jeans on Sunday' was probably her aunt's polite way of saying 'we dress for dinner.' She took down a pale gray skirt and a lilac sweater set. Imagine wearing clothes that matched your decor! It was like having a superhero costume, a signature look. She also found a pair of matching gray Keds. She rummaged around in the drawers and found some jewelry. Gray pearls will fit perfectly! She also found socks, underwear, gloves, hats, coats, and handbags. Maybe Phyllis was her fairy godmother! *Wait, who IS my godmother?* Lola thought, how did this question never occur to me? She always assumed it was Simone, but honestly, it was never discussed. She would broach the topic with Phyllis at dinner.

Setting her selections on the chaise, Lola moved on to the next door, which led to the en-suite bathroom. This was another large room, but this time with a glass shower, twin porcelain sinks, and a huge clawfoot tub. She grabbed a big, fluffy gray towel, stripped, and headed for the shower as it was getting late. She'd try the tub when she had more time to appreciate it truly.

Freshly scrubbed, Lola found an assortment of toiletries, all lilac scented and probably absurdly expensive. It made her feel like royalty! She put on the outfit she'd selected, did her hair, and added a little gloss to her lips. Her aunt must have known she wasn't one for makeup because she found none in the vanity. Only perfume and a lovely antique brush and comb set helped her curly hair become silky and bouncy. She was admiring herself in the full-length mirror when she heard a knock on the door. Glancing at her new watch, she saw it was only 5:45 p.m., and she wasn't running late. Perhaps Phyllis thought she might get lost on the way down.

But as she opened the door, she discovered it wasn't Phyllis looking back at her. Jackson, wearing dark gray slacks and, unbelievably, a lilac button-down shirt, open at the throat. Good lord, they were a matching set! She stared at him, open-mouthed. He looked gorgeous!

"Did my aunt choose your clothes too?" she blurted out.

"What? No! Why would you even ask that?" he replied, confused.

"Well, because we seem to match each other, and she bought these clothes for me," said Lola waving at herself.

"Pure coincidence." Jackson smiled at her. "You look nice, though. Are you ready to go down? Phyllis hates it when people are late to Sunday dinner," he said briskly.

"People?" Lola asked worriedly. "As in, there are other guests? I didn't even know *you'd* be there! Are you sure I look, okay?" asked Lola, a little insecure.

"You look fine, and it's only the three of us tonight. But sometimes there are friends of the family or neighbors that join us," he said calmly.

"Oh, okay then," Lola said, relieved. "Yes, I'm ready. Lead on!"

And with that, he offered her his arm, which she took with a giggle.

"How retro of you!" she exclaimed.

"The stairs can be a little tricky. And besides, your aunt expects it. Chivalry still has a place in the south and this house!" he said as he ushered her down the hall.

They walked down the stairs arm in arm, and Lola felt like a movie star. When they arrived in the formal dining room, her aunt was near the rollaway bar, drink in hand.

"Don't you look lovely, Lola!" she said with a smile.

"Thank you, Phyllis. The clothes and the room are amazing. Thank you so much!" Lola responded.

"My pleasure, dear. Truly. I haven't had this much fun in years! What can I get you to drink?" she asked, pointing at the cart.

"Um, I'm not old enough to drink," Lola said shyly.

"I know, silly! But we have sodas and juice, and I make a mean virgin margarita!" Phyllis chuckled.

"That sounds delicious!" Lola said gratefully.

"How about you, Jackson?" inquired Phyllis.

"I'll have a virgin Caesar, please," asked Jackson.

"Coming right up!" Phyllis replied.

They had drinks on the back terrace to watch the sunset and chatted amicably about local events. There was a dance coming up, and Phyllis thought Jackson should take Lola so she could meet some of the young people. She also mentioned Lola was looking for a job and asked if Jackson could take her to the Food Lion to introduce her to Mr. Xavier, the owner.

With those topics out of the way, they made their way into the dining room, where they found dishes laid out on the sideboard under heating lamps, and they served themselves. Lola's mouth began to water at the sight of the spread: roast beef, garlic, mashed potatoes with herbed butter, crispy green beans, and bacon. According to Phyllis, it was simple fare. Absolutely delicious, it was not Lola's usual Sunday meal, which usually consisted of store-bought rotisserie chicken and a green salad with fruit for dessert. Phyllis had made pecan pie served à la mode with homemade vanilla bean ice cream. Lola thought she was going to like it here!

CHAPTER 5
MANSION

AFTER DINNER, they had coffee on the front porch, and Phyllis talked about her father and growing up in this massive house.

She reminisced about her parents and Jackson's parents. Jackson also talked about his experience growing up on the property and how he wished he'd had siblings or friends that lived closer to play with on the huge grounds. Lola just listened. It felt good not to be the focus of attention. This was their shared history and hearing them talk made her feel like she had been there for it all. Eventually, they asked about her life in Baltimore, her school, her friends, and her mom. It seemed so boring compared to their stories. She'd only been here half a day, and life already had more meaning, more connection, more......life! She felt a little guilty like she was being disloyal to her mom. But then her thoughts started tumbling around in her head, and she wondered why she and her mom didn't move here with her dad. Or why she never visited him. But, of course, she knew the answer. Her father was unstable, and he died while she was still too young to travel so far to see him. She wondered if he had ever come to see her, and she just didn't remember it.

She realized she'd been lost in thought for a while when they stopped talking. She blushed and apologized and asked if they could repeat the question. It turned out there was no question, just a lull in the conversation. It was the perfect time to move on with their evening.

"Why don't you kids clear the table and put the dishes in the dishwasher? Marie will take care of the rest when she comes in tomorrow. Don't forget to add things you might need to the shopping list on the fridge and make sure your dirty laundry is in the hamper, or you'll be doing your own laundry! Jackson, be a dear and give Lola the grand tour of the house. You know it as well as I do, and perhaps even better. I'll head to the library for a nightcap. Come and say goodnight before you retire," Phyllis instructed.

"Sure thing, Phyllis," Jackson replied. "Come on, Lola."

They took care of business in the kitchen then set out for the tour that started in the basement. It was damp and dark and looked more like a castle dungeon than any basement Lola had ever visited. She was expecting storage, a laundry room, and maybe an old, noisy furnace. There was certainly a furnace, but also rows of dark, dank alcoves leading this way and that, and seemed much larger than the house, though it was hard to tell.

They didn't stay long, only long enough for Lola to know she had no reason to ever come down here again.

Next was the ground floor, which she was familiar with. In addition to the rooms she'd already visited, there was the laundry room, an access corridor to the three-car garage, the morning room, the glassed-in room Lola had seen on the picture, which held an impressive collection of herbs, plants, and flowers, a formal living room, and the library or study. That's where they found Phyllis curled up in an old leather armchair in front of a fire, sipping a glass of brandy, smoking a cigar, and reading War and Peace. Lola stood there, jaw hanging. Jackson knocked lightly on the door and entered, Lola trailing behind.

"Oh, hello, children, are you off to bed already?" she greeted them.

"No, we just started the first-floor tour," Jackson responded.

Phyllis put her book down and looked at the time. She frowned.

"Well, look at the time. Perhaps you should save the other floors for another day, Jackson," Phyllis advised.

"Alright, Phyllis," Jackson agreed. "It is getting late, and I have a few chores to attend to before turning in." He turned to Lola and added, "Lola, I'll have some time tomorrow afternoon to take you into town so that you can get your bearings, and then introduce you to Mr. Xavier at the Food Lion."

Lola thanked him, and he took his leave. She took in the library and its varied collection of works of fiction and non-fiction. There were a large oak desk and cabinet, where she assumed all the important household accounting took place. A large picture window beside it looked out over the grounds, though it was too dark to see much. Lola browsed the fiction section removed *The Great Gatsby, and* went to sit in the armchair next to her aunt. Her aunt cocked an eyebrow, silently asking what she'd chosen. When Lola showed her the cover, she nodded appreciatively and resumed her reading. They read in companionable silence for over an hour. At first, Lola was a bit self-conscious, but she was soon engrossed in the All-American novel, so much so that she gave a start when her aunt touched her gently on the arm and said she was turning in.

"What time is it?" Lola asked.

"It's only 9 p.m., but I have my nightly rituals to attend to," said Phyllis knowingly.

"Rituals?" Lola queried.

"You know, skincare, hair brushing, saying my prayers, that sort of thing."

"Oh, okay. Do you also go to church on Sundays?"

"No." Phyllis shook her head. "God and I have an understanding. But if you want to go to church, Jackson will take you next week. There are quite a few to choose from!" she said with a wink.

"No, I don't go to church, and I don't think I've said any prayers since I was five or six years old," Lola admitted sheepishly.

"Well, how about I say one for you tonight. Come on, I'll walk you to your room." And with that, Phyllis took her hand, and they went up the massive staircase. All Lola could think of was that old saying, 'When God closes one door, he always opens a window.' It would appear that Phyllis was her window.

CHAPTER 6
ROUTINE

LOLA WOKE up to a beautiful sunny day. She couldn't remember having ever slept so well or so soundly.

The light was streaming through the window, and she felt giddy with excitement over a new day, which wasn't like her at all. Until she remembered it was Monday. But it was also the summer vacation. No school! Then she took in her surroundings and wondered if she was dreaming. The gray and lilac decor, the king-sized bed, the fluffy pillows, and the extra-soft sheets. This couldn't be HER room, could it? But it was! How fortunate she had been to have not only a relative to take her in after her mom died, but a super nice one and wealthy to boot. These things just didn't happen in real life!

But apparently, they did. Lola got up, brushed her hair and teeth, and put on her new robe and slippers to go down to breakfast. She hoped she wasn't required to dress for that as well!

She followed the smell of coffee, rolls, and bacon to the sunroom but found it empty. On the table was a notecard with her name on it.

Good morning, Lola!

I hope you slept well! I'm afraid I won't be joining you for

> breakfast. I'm a bit of an early riser and have already eaten. Depending on the time, you'll either find me in the garden tending to my vegetables or under the gazebo for my morning yoga practice. Come and say hello when you are done.
>
> Phyllis
>
> XO

Lola went to the sideboard and peered at the spread: croissants, eggs, bacon, roasted potatoes, fresh fruit, cheese, orange juice, butter, and jam. And coffee, fragrant, hot, blessed coffee! With fresh cream. She was definitely going to like it here. But if she ate like this every day, she'd put on ten pounds in no time. Maybe she should ask her aunt about joining a gym or something. Or perhaps she could try yoga.

As she ate, she took in her surroundings. This was a less formal room but gorgeous, nonetheless. The flowery print in hues of yellow, green, and blue was a perfect backdrop to the sunny conservatory. The plants were mostly foreign to Lola, but she was never any good at botany, anyway, though they were pretty and fragrant.

She glanced outside and spotted Jackson on a tractor mowing the lawn. He was shirtless, and she could see he did physical labor every day; he was ripped! Unless he went to the gym, but he didn't seem like the jock type. Maybe he had a bench press in the garage. She'd have to find a discreet way to investigate. As though sensing he was being observed, Jackson looked towards the window and, seeing her there, gave a casual wave. She resisted the urge to step away from the window and pretend she hadn't just been gawking at him. It was pointless and immature, as he had obviously seen her. She waved back as nonchalantly as she could. Then she slowly walked away from the window and the sunroom in search of her aunt.

She found her in the garden, harvesting something into the large pockets of her apron. Clad in a wide brim sun hat, she looked every bit the part of the Lady Landowner.

"Are those going to be on tonight's menu?" she asked her aunt as she neared in the hopes of not startling her.

"I certainly hope so!" Phyllis replied. "But Marie is in charge of weekly meals, so you never can tell what she might come up with," she added.

"What have you collected?" asked Lola, peering into the apron.

"Okra, celery, a few cucumbers, parsnips, and a handful of asparagus!" replied her aunt proudly.

"Yum! I've never had okra, though I hear it's all the rage," said Lola a bit sarcastically.

Her aunt pretended to fan herself and replied with a thick, southern accent,

"Now, how is that even possible? You've been in the south for less than a day, and no one's offered you any collard greens, okra, or grits? Where is my southern hospitality?"

Lola cracked up at her aunt's southern belle routine and accent. She couldn't wait to go into town to see how pronounced the townies' accent was. It was so fascinating, like being in another country or something!

Her aunt transferred her loot to a large basket she had nearby. She took off her gloves and put her tools away in a small bin by the garden, and motioned Lola towards the house.

"Jackson should be done with his chores this morning and free to drive you around after lunch. Meanwhile, I thought we could get that tour done. It'll be good exercise going up and down those stairs!" said Phyllis.

"Sure, that sounds great, thanks," replied Lola.

And off they went arm in arm, like old friends. Phyllis left the basket in the kitchen with Marie and took a few minutes to introduce Lola. She cleaned up while Marie and Lola got acquainted and then headed to the second floor.

Lola's room was to the left and was basically the room above the foyer and main entrance. They started with the rooms on either side of her room. The first was an exercise room, or home gym, complete with a rower, a treadmill, and an elliptical, one of those structures for weight training like you see on tv, and a smaller room with wood floors wall of mirrors, and a ballet barre. *This must be where Phyllis does her yoga when the weather is foul.* There was even a water cooler and little rolled-up towels. It was an impressive set-up; she was sure to use it in the coming weeks.

The second room was simply a guest room, smaller than hers but just as beautiful. Decorated in hues of red and gold, it was almost regal. There was no tower, but there was a very welcoming window seat in the bay window. There was an en-suite bathroom but no walk-in closet, fireplace, or sitting room. Instead, an armoire and chest of drawers were provided for extended stays. There was also a matching writing desk and chair, as well as a pair of matching armchairs and a large table where two people could have tea or share a small breakfast tray. It truly was quite a lovely room and had Lola seen this one first, she would have been overjoyed at receiving such a well-appointed room. Not that she wanted to trade or anything!

"If there is a friend you'd like to invite over the summer, here is where he or she would stay," Phyllis remarked.

"He?" Lola said, blushing.

"I thought you might have a boyfriend......"

"No, no boyfriend," Lola said with a grin.

"Girlfriend?" tried Phyllis.

"No, I'm not into girls, but I do have a best friend, and she would go bonkers at the idea of staying here. Do you really mean it?" pleaded Lola.

"Yes, of course!" Phyllis' genuine caring shone through. "This is your home now. And though I'm certain you'll make new friends soon enough, you must miss your friends and the life you had in Baltimore," she said sympathetically.

"No one misses life in a small town on the outskirts of Baltimore. And I didn't have many friends. Only Jane." Lola's eyes grew wide, and she clasped her hands over her mouth. "O.M.G!" Lola exclaimed.

"What is it, dear?" Phyllis asked worriedly.

"I completely forgot! I was supposed to call Jane when I got here, or at the very least check my email, and I completely zoned out. And since I didn't know if you had Wi-Fi or not, I didn't even open my iPad," explained Lola breathlessly.

"Well, it hasn't even been twenty-four hours; I'm sure she understands you've been busy. But go ahead and call her, if you like. I can wait. And yes, we do have Wi-Fi. The password is RODENT," said Phyllis with a wink.

"Rodent?" Lola responded in surprise.

"It was Jackson's choice. We take turns coming up with funny names to confuse would-be hackers!"

"Ha-ha, that's funny! Well, if you don't mind, I could just send her a quick email to tell her I'll call her later when I have time for a proper chat. Back in a flash!" said Lola, already out the door.

"As you wish," called Phyllis after her.

CHAPTER 7

TOUR

LOLA LITERALLY RAN BACK to her room while Phyllis closed up the guest room. She barely had time to have a seat on the hallway bench when Lola came back and skidded to a stop in front of her.

Phyllis burst out laughing. "You really meant in a flash! All right, then, let's continue with the tour," said Phyllis, still chuckling.

Across the hall from the guest room was what Phyllis called the nursery. It was a huge room! On the back wall, it had two sets of custom-built, full-size bunk beds, end-to-end but separated by a small staircase and built-in cabinets that opened inside each bunk bed so that the occupant could store their clothing at the foot of their bed. At the head of the beds was a small, encased alcove with two shelves for books or toys, an electrical outlet, and a reading lamp. Each bed also had three drawers underneath for additional storage. To match the nautical theme, each bed had its very own porthole window. It was ingenious! The beds looked sturdy and comfortable enough to hold full-grown adults. Lola could imagine having a sleep-over in this room! On the opposite wall were a huge flat-screen TV and a long four-seater sofa that ended with a chaise on either end. There was enough room for six to watch a movie or show and space for two more guests to sleep on. Upon looking up, Lola saw the ceiling had been painted to resemble clouds and was dotted with hundreds of little yellow stars, which Lola knew would glow in the dark at night.

"Was this your room as a child?" asked Lola.

"No, I'm still in the room I had as a child. However, our mother and her brother stayed in the nursery when they were children, as did most Evers children throughout the ages. After your father died, when it became apparent, I was not going to have children, I had the room redecorated to accommodate the children of guests who might visit or children and grandchildren of the next generation. It was such fun to do! Come and see the schoolroom and the playroom!" Phyllis was obviously enjoying herself, and she took Lola's hand and pulled her along.

"Schoolroom?" asked Lola.

"Back in the day, wealthy people were taught at home by a governess, and later tutors. I tried to keep the essence of the room," said Phyllis.

They walked through a short, narrow hall. On one side was a regular-sized bathroom with a double sink, a toilet, and a tub-shower combo. On the other side were two closets. The room beyond was indeed a schoolroom! It had a white smart board connected to a computer on the *teacher's desk* and two large library-type tables, each with six chairs. This class could easily hold twelve students! On the far side was a counter with a sink with a window above. The counter was full of chemistry and biology equipment, and the cabinets below had various school and art supplies. The rest of the walls that were not covered with floor-to-ceiling bookcases held a variety of large posters such as the periodic table, a world map, and detailed anatomy and astronomy sketches. The room wasn't that big, but it was well organized and didn't feel stuffy. Lola was impressed.

"Oh. My. God! This place is state of the art!" she exclaimed.

"Do you really like it?" asked Phyllis hopefully.

"Of course, who wouldn't?" Lola said in awe.

"I was thinking that unless you've got your heart set on going to school and meeting new friends there, you might consider learning from home. Either online, or I could hire tutors to come in periodically.

You only have a year left. Of course, you wouldn't get the whole senior year experience and prom......" trailed Phyllis.

"Yes, yes, yes! I don't care about all that other stuff. I was actually trying to find a way out of going to prom next year without looking like a total loser! Besides, I could still go to prom at my old school if I was desperate enough," said Lola in a rush.

"Well, that's settled. Let me know how you want to proceed, and we'll set it up," said Phyllis, clasping her hands in delight.

"Maybe a combination of online and in-person tutors, I'd say," Lola mused. "I'm a bit of a loner and tend to learn best by myself, but some things, like French and Spanish, are hard to do and require frequent practice around others," she added.

"You, young lady, are in luck! I am fluent in French, Italian, Catalan, and German! Spanish, however, is not my strong suit," declared Phyllis.

"Wow! Do you also play the piano, the cello, and dance ballet?" asked Lola innocently.

Phyllis put a hand to her heart said, "How did you know?"

"I was being sarcastic." Lola chuckled. "You're way too accomplished. You're like those ladies in a Jane Austen novel," she added.

Phyllis nodded in agreement. "I had far too much time on my hands as a child. My parents were always afraid to let me roam outside at leisure unless Simon was with me. But he was always painting, mostly inside. Getting him to play with me out-of-doors was like pulling teeth. I passed the time with solitary pursuits." Phyllis sighed.

"Because of your epilepsy? Couldn't you take pills or something?" inquired Lola.

Phyllis patted Lola's hand and motioned for her to follow as she replied.

"I do now. But back then, it was still very experimental. And some people even believed I was possessed by the devil! Thus, I learned to keep to myself and enjoy my own company."

"That's so sad!" Lola exclaimed.

"Are you sad?" Phyllis responded.

"No, why?" Lola said, puzzled.

"Well, you have no siblings, and you keep to yourself too," said Phyllis.

"You're right! And though I was able to go outside as a child, my mother had to strong-arm me out of the house and banish me to the playground until dinner time. Otherwise, I would have stayed inside reading books all day!" said Lola with a laugh.

"But did you enjoy the playground?" asked Phyllis as they were back in the nursery proper and heading towards a similar hall at the other end of the room. Everything was so symmetrical! It was somehow soothing. This passage had an identical bathroom and two closets but opened up onto the playroom.

"No, it was awful. All those screaming kids! Then, one day, I met Jane, who always wore pretty dresses and was afraid to get them dirty. She sat on the bench until her mother came to get her. She looked as bored as I felt. I went over and introduced myself, and we've been friends ever since! Eventually, we figured out we could go to the public library for most of the day, then come back and sit on the swings until it was time to go home," said Lola, smiling at the memory.

Phyllis laughed in delight and exclaimed, "How clever of you!" as she paused just inside the playroom.

Near the window, there was a large table with six chairs—presumably used for board games, card games, or puzzles. In the middle of the room was a huge carpet with the entire solar system as a backdrop. Two walls were lined with deep cabinets full of toys, puzzles, and games. The last wall held another large TV screen, with hanging shelves below it on which a soundbar and subwoofer, as well as the better-known game consoles, sat. Kids of any age would flip for this room!

"It's too bad you didn't have any kids. They would love it here!" The enthusiasm in Lola's voice shone through.

"I've had a few guests over who had kids of varying ages, and they all seemed to enjoy themselves. The parents enjoyed it too, in the sense that they got a break from their children for hours at a time!" replied Phyllis.

They left the nursery and walked down the hall. Next to the guest room was a huge bedroom, larger than Lola's but similar in design. This room also had a tower, but it was wider, with a wrought-iron staircase leading to an art studio. This must have been her father's room. She looked back at Phyllis, who nodded, and she went up to see the studio. The tower was the perfect place for a studio because it had windows all around and was set on a corner of the house that ensured sunlight from early morning to early afternoon. There were stacks of finished and unfinished paintings under the windows; one of the unfinished pieces was on the easel, as though waiting for the artist to resume painting. Lola would have thought that this particular room would have been left untouched, like a shrine. But strangely, there was no dust anywhere. As Phyllis joined her in the studio, Lola asked, "What was he like, my dad?"

Phyllis thought for a moment, trailing her hand along the edges of portraits, and walked around admiring her brother's legacy. "Simon was an artist. Even as a child, you could always tell he was off in his own little world. As you can see, he was quite talented. But he could never part with any of his paintings. It's a shame because he could have earned a good living with it, out in the real world," she said with a sigh.

"I wish he had felt the same way about me. He parted with me pretty easily, it seems—" blurted Lola before putting a hand on her mouth, shamefaced. "I'm so sorry. I don't know what came over me!"

"Oh dear, don't apologize. You obviously don't know the whole story, and in that case, your reaction is quite understandable. Let me explain," Phyllis cooed. "You should know your father did not part with you easily. He wanted to bring you home with him when he left. But neither of us knew anything about raising a child, and besides, you were much too young to be separated from your mother. He planned on requesting visitation as you got older, but, unfortunately, time was not on his side. Your father loved you very much. In fact, he left you a letter! It's right here!" said Phyllis as she pointed to it.

On a table, next to a reading chair, was indeed a letter with her name on it. As if someone had placed it there only moments ago. But her father had been dead now for thirteen years. Surely it would have gathered dust or yellowed and curled with age?

Seeing the confusion on her face, Phyllis added, "He gave it to me for safekeeping and asked me to give it to you when you came. Whenever that may be. I put it here this morning, knowing we would have our tour. How about you have a seat and read it while I go see about lunch? We've been inside a very long time; join me on the back terrace when you're ready. Okay?"

Phyllis gave her niece a quick hug and left Lola alone with her father's letter.

CHAPTER 8
LETTER

Feelings were whirling inside Lola. Trepidation, fear, anger, joy. She was all over the place.

She took a deep breath, exhaled slowly, and eased down into the chair. It had a faint smell of pipe tobacco though she couldn't see a pipe or ashtray nearby. Gingerly, she took the envelope and looked at it. Her name was handwritten with a rather flowery hand in long, sure strokes. An artist indeed! She turned the envelope over and saw it was sealed with wax and stamped S.E. for Simon Evers. Her father. As she held it, she felt a lump inside the envelope and shook it slightly. There was something inside other than a letter!

Quickly but gently, she lifted the wax seal and peered into the envelope. Inside, the folds of a three-page letter were a rose gold chain and matching locket. Opening it, she saw a picture of the three of them when she was a baby. Her parents were beaming at the camera, proud parents of a perfect infant girl. Her heart leaped at the sight of it, as she had never seen this picture before. Proof that she had once had a set of happy parents! On the other side of the locket was a sepia-colored family portrait of Phyllis, Simon, and their parents. The kids must have been about six and eight. Phyllis is in pigtails and one tooth missing; Simon smiling proudly at the camera with an arm around his sister.

Their parents—Belva and Morris, she would later learn—held hands with one hand and the other resting on the children's shoulders. Belva on Simon's; Morris on Phyllis.' It was a good photograph and an attractive family. Lola looked at the children to see if she resembled either of them but could not tell. She'd have to compare her own pictures at that age to be sure.

She closed the locket with a snap and fastened the chain around her neck. The locket settled between her breasts, resting against her heart. *What a wonderful gift.*

Next, she held the letter out in front of her like a scroll. The paper was thick and heavy. She unfolded the pages and saw the same beautiful handwriting, and her heart skipped a beat. A letter from her father! How she dreamed of this moment! The top of each page was embossed with her father's initials but had no other markings. She began to read.

September 9, 2002

My Dearest Lola,

As I write these lines, you are miles and miles away, safe in your mother's arms. I am here, in my studio, pen in hand, ready to write my final words. You see, I'm ill. Very ill. That's why I left. As not to burden your mother with taking care of an ailing husband as well as a young child. Cancer came upon me like a thief in the night. Robbing me of my family, my health, and, eventually, of my mind. It took everything I had to leave you, please know that. I loved you then and love you still. I will love you forever. That's what we Evers do. We love forever. I will always love your mother. She is upset with me, I know, and will be more so when I pass. I stayed for as long as we were able to enjoy normal days and nights together. When I started coughing blood, I knew it was time to go.

Your mother sends me letters and pictures regularly. How you've grown! I'm sure by now you've turned into an amazing young woman. If you are reading this, it means your mother has permitted you to visit your Aunt Phyllis, or you have turned eighteen and have come on your own. Either way, welcome! This is your home. I mean that quite literally. This is YOUR home. As you are my only child and heir, it will be yours when I pass. Dispositions in the will have been included so that Phyllis may live out her days here as well, just like our parents did. It's the Evers way. Evers are always welcome in the family home, no matter who owns it. ***Evers are Forever****.*

Until you reach twenty-one, your Aunt Phyllis will manage the house and all the accounts. Your mother requested that you not be informed of these terms until you turned eighteen, and we have respected her wishes.

Now that you are in the house, you might realize the scope of our wealth. Know that it will enable you to be, do, or have anything your heart desires. But it won't be enough. You'll need the strength of character, wisdom, courage, and compassion to truly live an exceptional life. Remember that while you have the resources to make all your dreams come true, you also have the responsibility to help others achieve theirs too.

In my nightstand, you'll find the old family bible. There, you will see our family tree. It goes back to 1620! When the time comes, your aunt will acquaint you with the running of the house and the accounts. You are not required to take on these tasks yourself or even to live in the home until Phyllis dies. After this, it will be a requirement. There has always been an Evers in residence, and one day, that will be you and your husband, your children, and, if you are luckier than Phyllis and I, your grandchildren.

Phyllis will also tell you about our ancestors and the particular family quirks that have been passed down from generation to generation. Don't worry, there are no cases of mental illnesses in our family, and other than me and the early settlers, most of our ancestors died of old age.

Darling girl, know that I will watch over you from wherever I am. Love transcends Time and Space. Enjoy your life, and make it a good one. Take risks, open your heart, and stay true to yourself, and you'll be just fine.

With all my Love,

Dad

Lola sat with the letter in her hand, tears rolling down her cheeks. He loved her! He had always loved her! He loved her still, always, and forever. Oh, how she wished she had known him, wished he was here now to take her in his arms. She felt so alone. Yet she knew she should be grateful for his gift—his legacy. For Phyllis, the house and the fresh start.

Lola jumped as she felt a hand on her shoulder. Thinking it was her aunt coming to check up on her, she rose without looking and came face to face with Jackson. She felt vulnerable and exposed, but she just didn't have the energy to put on a brave front. His face was calm and understanding, so Lola just launched herself into a hug. His arms moved around her and held her tight. He didn't say anything, just held her. When she eventually leaned away from him, embarrassed, he took a tissue and wiped her eyes. When she said nothing, he said that lunch was ready, but if she needed to talk, or be left alone, or to have a tray sent up, he was there for her.

She smiled, blew her nose noisily, and thanked him. "I'm hungry, and the fresh air and sunshine should lift my spirits." And so, they went down to lunch.

At lunch, Phyllis announced she needed a ride into town because Betty at the music store had received a new shipment and had called to give Phyllis first dibs. She announced she would take the afternoon to pay her respects to her local acquaintances and that the kids should take the opportunity to visit the town and look in on the Food Lion. Lola was feeling self-conscious after her little meltdown, so she said nothing. But Jackson was all for it and started chattering about all the places he wanted to take her. After a bit, he turned to her and asked if she wanted to go or if she preferred to stay and get settled in. His enthusiasm was infectious, and it put her at ease. He obviously didn't hold her meltdown against her, or he was being a really decent guy. Either way, she was going to take him up on his offer!

CHAPTER 9

POSSUM

AFTER LUNCH, Jackson left to get the car while Phyllis and Lola got their purses. The car, a black Bentley no less, pulled up in front of the house as they were closing the door. Jackson exited the vehicle and came around to open the door for the ladies. Lola blushed and giggled when Jackson said, "Your car, madam." She and Phyllis sat in the back, and Jackson resumed his chauffeur duties. As he left the private lane and merged onto the road, he winked at Lola in the mirror. She blushed again and tried to focus on the scenery.

The drive to town took about fifteen minutes. It was closer than Lola thought. Phyllis, and now her, lived in a semi-rural part of the town, and her neighbors, such as they were, had not kept up with repairs as well as the Evers household had. The neighborhood had somewhat of a rundown, old manor, creepy feeling to it. In fact, the closest neighbor must be at least three miles away. Well, in the direction they had headed anyway. Maybe the other neighbor was close. How did Phyllis stand to be so far away from everyone? *I'm a loner and all, but I can go places and see people. Phyllis is, or at least she was, home alone. If the power was out, and Jackson was gone, and there was an emergency, what would she do?*

"Take a look at this house, Lola," said Phyllis. "It's been here almost as long as ours, and they've done a lovely job with the upkeep. It's a shame it didn't stay in the family, though. The Fentons were descendants of John Fenton, one of the original settlers of Williamsburg in 1607," said Phyllis knowledgeably.

Lola looked at the huge mansion in wonder as they passed it. It, too, had a long lane lined with trees, so she only caught a glimpse. "Wow. You mean they came right off the boat and started building?" she asked.

"Just about," replied Phyllis. "They settled in Williamsburg where dwellings were already established, and a few years later, like the Evers, they were given land in exchange for their loyalty to the Crown. Roads were built, supplies were brought, and in 1620, our little town was born."

"That's amazing! And a lot more interesting than any history class I've ever had. Perhaps you could be my history teacher, and likely my dance master too," quipped Lola.

At this, Jackson piped up, "You can dance?"

"No, that's why I need a dance master. I can be an accomplished young lady and have a proper coming out when I turn sixteen," said Lola sarcastically.

But clearly, her tone was lost on Jackson as he replied, "Are you serious? There's no way you'll have time! The events are booked months in advance, you don't have a dress, and it's what, like two weeks until your birthday, so you'll never have enough time to learn how to dance!" he said with an appalled look on his face.

Lola stared at him open-mouthed. Phyllis was trying not to laugh, but it was hard to tell if she was laughing at his passionate speech or the fact that he wasn't joking.

"What?" Lola spluttered. "I was kidding! Are you saying these things actually still exist?"

"Yes, of course, there is a cotillion in mid-July," he replied without missing a beat.

"Oh. My. God. That is so retro!" exclaimed Lola.

Phyllis was chuckling. But Jackson seemed to be taking this entirely too earnestly. "Retro?" he nearly shouted. "Have you forgotten you're in the south? People take this sort of thing very seriously. And being from one of the most prominent families not only in town but in the state, you have a responsibility to do your family proud and represent them at social events." He concluded by tapping on the steering wheel as though it was a proclamation.

Lola couldn't believe what she was hearing. She turned to Phyllis, either for confirmation of these facts or affirmation that Jackson was totally off his rocker, but Phyllis was staring at her hands in her lap.

"Phyllis, is this what's expected of me?" Lola said in a panic.

"Well, dear, there's really no expectation. Had you been brought up in the house, you would have been prepared for this sort of thing, and it wouldn't sound quite so dated as I'm sure it does. This type of socializing lets prominent families introduce their youngsters to their social equals in the hopes they may form lasting bonds. Should they choose to marry, the families would be overjoyed, but it's not expected or arranged," Phyllis reassured her.

"Oh good," Lola said, relieved. "Here, I thought you were about to announce I was betrothed at birth, and you were really taking me to his house like chattel," she said, trying, but failing, to relax.

Phyllis and Jackson exchanged a look and said nothing. At the very least, Lola thought they would laugh at her outrageous suggestion. But their silence was unsettling.

"What are you not telling me? I've already found out I'm expected to have children and live in the house forever. Please tell me there isn't more," she pleaded.

"Lola, of course, when you put it that way, it sounds terrible. But you're quite fortunate," replied Jackson.

"I'm sorry, you're right. I'm being ungrateful. It's just a lot to take in." Lola sank in her seat, closed her eyes, and took deep breaths. Phyllis put a hand on her shoulder.

"I understand, dear. I'm not upset, and I certainly didn't mean to upset you. The truth is, my mother was very fond of Jackson's parents and always hoped you, and he would end up together," Phyllis said simply.

"But, I mean, well......"..." she trailed off, confused and unable to find a tactful way of saying Jackson was not from a wealthy or prominent family. She certainly didn't care, and she was pretty sure most people outside the town of Possum didn't give a rat's ass about it. As though reading her mind, Phyllis continued. "Jackson's family are descendants of Richard Dixon," she said. "Another of Williamsburg's first settlers. The Dixons were a well-respected family until the end of the Civil War in 1866 when Horace Dixon gambled away the family fortune, and they were obligated to sell the family home because they couldn't afford the upkeep of the house, or the staff required to tend it. Horace drank himself to death. His wife and female children went to live with relatives, while the boys were sent to live with other prominent families so that they may be educated as gentlemen and have a chance at a rosier future. The elder son, Jonathan, aged fifteen, was sent to the Cooke's. He later became a barrister and was able to purchase a parcel of land, marry the youngest daughter of one of the founding families, and did quite well for himself. The youngest son, Jacob, aged twelve, fell in love with one of the maids at the Estate he was sent to. When he turned eighteen, they married, and he took over as caretaker of the Estate. When the house burned down in 1896, he, his wife, and two children came to live with my great-grandparents. The Dixons have been our caretakers ever since. So, they are neither wealthy nor prominent, but they are a worthy family, to be sure," concluded Phyllis.

Lola was listening intently. Phyllis was an excellent storyteller, and for a minute, Lola forgot she was talking about real people—specifically Jackson's family. "Wow, that's quite a story! And I didn't mean any disrespect. I mean, before I came here, I was considering working at Starbucks as a career choice......" trailed Lola.

Jackson started laughing, as did Phyllis. Soon Lola joined them, and the tension in the car eased somewhat.

"Please tell me this was just the fervent wish of an old romantic matron and not an iron-clad contract signed in one of the dungeons under the house?" Lola begged with a tight smile.

"Dungeons?" spluttered Phyllis. "Jackson, what exactly have you been telling the poor girl?"

"Nothing! I showed her the basement. It's dark and dank, so I'm assuming her imagination came up with the part about dungeons. I swear!" replied Jackson with a chuckle.

But they were saved from pursuing the topic when Jackson drove up to Betty's Music Store. They all got out so Phyllis could introduce Lola to her friend. In the end, they walked the village with Phyllis for over an hour so she could show off her new niece. Phyllis was beaming with pride. Look at my brother's daughter, all grown up, her expression seemed to imply. Lola wasn't used to this much attention, but she grinned and bore it as it was giving her aunt so much pleasure, and people didn't ask too many questions. With such a small town, they probably knew her whole life story by now, anyway.

Phyllis eventually cut them loose, and they took the car to drive around town to see the high school, the churches, the Town Hall, the Police and Fire departments, and the library. Lola asked if they could go and check it out.

"Really? I think there are more books in the Evers' library than in the town library!" Jackson commented.

"Please? We won't stay long. You can tell a lot about a place by the library and the books it carries," Lola pleaded.

"Oh! You're a book nerd! Now I get it!" said Jackson, rolling his eyes.

Lola punched him in the arm and started towards the steps.

CHAPTER 10
LIBRARY

IT WAS a typical Virginian brick building with white columns in the center. Next to the massive entry was a neat sign reading Possum Public Library. This was promising!

Upon entering, Lola was immediately hit by the unique smell one can only find in a very old library. She looked towards the counter, expecting an ancient librarian with rusty spectacles. But there was no one. She walked towards the stacks and started peering at the shelves. Did anyone read in this town? The books looked like they hadn't been dusted in over fifty years. Then again, this was the history and geography section. Perhaps they had a better selection at the high school, and students didn't use these books for reference. She walked on, going from one section to another, and finally made it to the fiction area. She was just turning the corner, following the letters to find an author she liked, when she heard a whooshing sound, a screech, and the sound of multiple books crashing to the floor.

"Son of a Motherless Goat! Where in Sam Hill did you come from?" cried out a girl who promptly crashed into a shelf of books and fell down.

Lola stared at the girl on the floor. She had rollerblades on and was trying to assemble a stack of books she must have been returning to the shelves when she fell. Jackson jogged up, took the books, and helped her up.

"Lola, meet Bonnie, the assistant librarian. She works here in the summer and on weekends during the school year while she finishes her degree. She hopes to take over for Miss Langley when she retires. Bonnie, this is Lola, Phyllis' niece from Baltimore," said Jackson.

"Mr. Evers' daughter?" Bonnie asked.

"Yes, that's right," Lola replied.

"Oh, how nice to meet you! I'm so sorry to hear about your mom," said Bonnie sympathetically.

"Um, thanks, I guess," replied Lola awkwardly, shuffling her feet.

"Do you want a tour of the library? It's not much to look at right now, but when I get full run of the place, it'll be amazing!" said Bonnie a little too gleefully.

Jackson took this as his cue to go grab a magazine and get comfortable in the armchairs by the fire. Bonnie took Lola around and showed her the usual areas and sections, as well as the computers designated for personal use and those used to search for books. At the far back end of the library was a small room with a window looking in but no window opening to the outside. Lola stopped and peered through the glass. The walls were lined with floor-to-ceiling bookcases with a sliding ladder to get to the upper shelves. They seemed to be filled with old leather-bound books of varying shapes and sizes. There was a small table with a couple of chairs in the middle. Lola could just imagine how *those* books would smell! She turned the knob on the door only to find it locked. She turned her puppy-eyed gaze to Bonnie and said, "I just want to smell them. I promise I won't touch a thing!" Bonnie laughed and explained this room was for first editions and only the Librarian had the key.

Lola was clearly bummed, but Bonnie launched into a very interesting narrative on how researchers tried to develop ways to characterize, preserve, and ultimately recreate old book smells. By analyzing the volatile organic compounds, or VOCs, emitted by books in a lab, they captured those compounds and used a mass spectrometer to analyze its chemical signature. Lola learned that since books are made of paper,

.i.e., wood, and are constantly decomposing, they release chemical compounds into the air that mix together to form a unique scent. One so dear to Lola's heart. Fascinated, Lola completely forgot about the room as she listened intently to Bonnie.

"Wow! You know your stuff!" she exclaimed. Bonnie blushed and apologized for going nerdy on them. "Don't worry," said Lola. "I'm really into books and libraries too. Where do you go to school?" she asked with genuine interest.

"I just finished my second year of Library Science at Old Dominion University, in Norfolk. It's about an hour away. I could commute, but my grandparents live right on Ocean View Beach, so I stay with them during the week. It's a sweet deal!" explained Bonnie as she took them to her favorite spot—a handful of armchairs all lined up in front of a massive fireplace. Lola was about to comment on how cool it was for her to live on the beach when she did a double take looking at the fireplace. The thing was so big all three of them could have stepped into the firebox.

"How long does it take to light that thing?" Lola enquired.

"It must have taken hours back in the day, but they converted it to gas a few years ago for safety reasons. It's on all day, every day. It reduces the humidity and gives the library a nice, cozy feel, don't you agree?" asked Bonnie.

"Yes, but doesn't it get hot over the summer?" asked Lola.

"There's an electrical component as well which provides the illusion of fire and crackling, but without the heat. That's what we use in the summer months. In spring and fall, if things heat up, I try to open a few windows for ventilation, but as you can see, not many of them open. Most are sealed shut with years of paint. It's one of the first things I'll recommend. Large, new windows to let the light in! And a new central heating and cooling system to maintain a constant level of humidity. It's really important for book preservation."

"Yes, that would be an improvement," agreed Lola.

"Well, you certainly didn't come here to hear me chatting all day. Would you like to register for a library card?" inquired Bonnie.

"Yes, please! But I don't have proof of residence yet," added Lola.

"Heavens to Betsy, you have better! You're the heir and youngest descendant of one of the founding families. You'll have no trouble getting anything you want in this town," said Bonnie, waving her objections away. Lola just stood there, feeling incredibly uncomfortable by the comment, and had no idea how to respond. But Bonnie was clearly not bothered by it and had already gone back to the counter.

They got her card done in no time. Lola was half expecting a handwritten card with a double in a Rolodex, but the library records had been computerized in the early nineties and later updated when the Internet was made widely available. Her card was the generic type with a barcode on one side, and Possum Public Library printed on the other. Bonnie warned her not to lose it, or it would cost $5 to replace it. Lola gave a discreet *psst* to catch Jackson's attention, waving her new card at him as if she'd just been given the keys to the city. Jackson smiled and rose to join her at the counter. And with that, they left the library. Lola promised to return when she had more time to browse and chat. She had made a friend!

CHAPTER 11
JOB

NEXT, they went to the Food Lion to meet the famous Mr. Xavier. He was very friendly and gave Lola a form to fill out. She apologized for not having a resume handy, and he only laughed at that. He said resumes were for city folk who don't shake on it while looking at each other in the eye. She said she was available all summer and would get back to him later about her fall schedule.

"How about we give it a week, young lady, and see how we both feel about it?" he said.

"Sure, that sounds fair," agreed Lola.

"When can you start?" he asked.

"Anytime, but I'll have to check with my driver here," replied Lola with a shake of the head at Jackson.

"Jackson? He's got a very loose schedule, I can tell you that!" responded Mr. Xavier with a chuckle.

"Does he now? Well, he certainly has the best boss ever, am I right?" quipped Lola.

"Miss Evers is the salt of the earth, that's for darn sure! Jackson, can you have her back here at 1 p.m. every day this week? I'll keep her until 5 p.m. I'm here early every morning for deliveries, and after you've gotten used to the place, I could get some paperwork done in the back or leave early to spend time with my grandkids! I've got someone who covers nights and weekends. How does that sound?" asked Mr. Xavier.

Both Lola and Jackson agreed. Mr. Xavier and Lola arranged to discuss her schedule later in the week if they decided to pursue their professional relationship. Lola was giddy with excitement; her first job! Jackson laughed at her clapping her hands and jumping up and down.

"We'll see how you feel on Friday. It's not that great of a job!" Jackson warned her.

"Who cares!" said Lola delightedly. "I'll earn my own money and have something to add to my resume other than babysitting!" said Lola excitedly.

"But you and Phyllis are wealthy, and besides, it's your house and your money!" countered Jackson.

"I know, but it feels wrong that it should be mine when I didn't do anything to earn it except being born," replied Lola.

"That's the way things work in wealthy families. I think that's the way things should work all the time. Being born should be enough," said Jackson, his voice rising with each word.

"But how would people learn about hard work?" Lola could feel the beginning of an argument brewing. They were outside on the sidewalk by now, heading towards the car, but Lola stopped and stared at him in frustration.

"People don't learn about hard work through strife and misery. They work a lot harder when they are going after their dreams. But poor and hungry people don't have time to dream. They're too busy surviving!" said Jackson passionately. He was waving his arms about him and had a fierce look on his face. It made Lola nervous, and when she was nervous, she either babbled or burst out laughing. She did the latter. Jackson was not amused, and she felt like a heel.

"Wow, you really take this seriously," said Lola cautiously.

"Yes, I do. And so should you. You're about to be put into a position of wealth, power, and influence. You could really change things if you wanted to," he said, lowering his voice and speaking a little more calmly.

"That's a little intense," Lola said with a gulp. "I'm only fifteen years old. What can I do?"

Jackson put his hands through his hair, took a breath and put his hands together, and tapped his mouth lightly, pondering how to respond. Then he put his hands on Lola's shoulders and replied, "I'm sorry, you're right. I'm being much too hard on you, and this has to be really overwhelming for you. But if you'd been raised here from childhood, you'd already be engaged in numerous charitable ventures," he explained. Jackson dropped his hands from Lola's shoulders and took a step back. He motioned for them to keep walking.

"Ladies-who-lunch, you mean?" said Lola sarcastically.

"Something like that, but they don't just spend their days in fancy restaurants and talk about their pets or the latest decorations. You'll notice that Possum is not overrun with those. However, the wealthy and powerful ladies of Williamsburg hold the keys to the social and economic growth in the South," stated Jackson.

"Is that what Phyllis does?" asked Lola.

"No, Phyllis keeps to herself. Since your father and her parents have passed, she's been investing money to make the Estate grow, and she gives annually to several local and regional charities, but that's about it." They got to a street corner and waited for the crosswalk. Seeing a small park across the street, Lola asked if they could go sit on a bench to continue this conversation. Jackson agreed, and soon they were crossing the street and settling in for a chat. "I mean, she still attends major functions, but she's not a social butterfly or anything." Jackson turned on the bench to face her and draped an arm against the back of the bench. "When my parents died, and I came back here, I took over the books. But she's still the boss," he added.

Lola, cross-legged and facing Jackson, didn't respond immediately while she pondered what he had just said. Jackson seemed to be staring off into space, or maybe at something happening behind her. Either way, it seemed a good time to observe him a little more closely. He wasn't just a handsome boy. He was mature, with adult responsibilities which he clearly took seriously, and with great commitment. To get his attention, she lightly touched his arm as she asked, "Well, how would you do things differently?"

He turned and looked at her and smiled like he was really happy that she had asked. "If it was my money, I'd invest it in technologies and programs that help people lead better, richer lives. We may have abolished slavery decades ago, but we only replaced it with another type of slavery. Financial slavery. Money controls people. Without it, they cannot strive. Some people have managed to get off the grid and return to the simpler life of their ancestors. They grow their own food, make their own clothes, and get electricity from solar panels. They are free of the system, but all their time is put into surviving, so it amounts to the same thing. They are slaves to time. They have none of it to enjoy, to pursue their passions, to just be. We need the idleness of youth to truly be happy, to appreciate life on this amazing planet," Jackson explained.

"I never thought about it that way. It's exciting to think about!" said Lola, impressed by the breadth of Jackson's knowledge and the passion he seemed to have for the topic.

"If you want, I can show you some books and articles that discuss the kind of initiatives I'd implement and how they've succeeded in other countries," added Jackson.

"I'd like that, thanks," said Lola with genuine interest.

Jackson looked at his watch and brought the conversation to a halt. "We should get back to Main Street. It's almost time to pick Phyllis up."

CHAPTER 12
HOME

AS THEY WALKED BACK, Lola asked Jackson if he could teach her to drive, and he agreed. She would need the freedom of being able to drive herself to where she wanted to go soon enough, and she had plenty of time over the summer to get this chore done. Even if she chose to be homeschooled, it would be convenient to have an extra driver in the house so Phyllis wouldn't rely so heavily on Jackson. It was one way she could give back to both of them.

They found Phyllis in the town rotunda, chatting with a few ladies at the end of Main Street. It was the central part of downtown. Four roads led to it as though to ensure people would always find their way back. It was a lovely little town if a little old, and some of the shops were dated and a bit run down. It had a very authentic feeling, though. People seemed to know and appreciate one another. And Phyllis seemed well-loved despite her reclusiveness.

They walked over to see her, and she introduced Lola to her friends. They were all delighted to meet with her and mentioned that they had daughters her age who would also love to meet her. Jackson suggested that the upcoming dance could be a good time for introductions.

They took their leave and walked back to the car. Jackson stopped to pick up a few packages at the shops Phyllis had visited, and then they were on their way home. Phyllis asked Lola about her first impressions of the town, the places she'd visited, and the people she'd met. Lola told her about Bonnie and her new job at the Food Lion, and Phyllis seemed pleased.

SOON THEY WERE HOME, and they went their separate ways. Phyllis promised to finish the—second-floor tour the next day after dinner.

Lola went back to her room and, seeing she had plenty of time before dinner, decided to use the house phone to call Jane and tell her all about her first day. Had it only been twenty-four hours? It didn't seem possible that so many things could change and happen in such a short time. They chatted for well over an hour. Jane told her about going to prom with Jason, a senior she had a crush on but who hadn't made any formal overtures towards her before prom. Now she thought they might be dating, but it was too soon to tell.

Then came the bits about Jackson, her aunt, the house, and the town, but she left out the massive wealth and responsibilities that came with it. She also mentioned that Jane could come to stay for a while whenever she was free—if her mom agreed, of course. They made plans for Jane to come for the 4th of July weekend, as it was also near Lola's birthday, on the 6th. Jane would take a few days off work at Walmart, and the girls could spend four days together. Lola couldn't wait to show Jane her room and the house. She was sure Jane wouldn't be jealous but would instead be happy for her. Lola and her mom had struggled for so long to make ends meet. This type of affluence almost seemed indecent. Almost.

As Lola showered, she counted her blessings. When she got out and looked for something to wear, even though dressing up was not required on a weeknight, she decided to pay homage to those blessings. Tonight, she chose another skirt. She'd never been into girly apparel, but these skirts and dresses were gorgeous and comfortable, and the fabrics were so soft. It was like wearing your favorite robe all day. This skirt was indigo blue, and she wore it with a silk floral print blouse with three-quarter sleeves that had a simple V-neck with no collar. She found earrings to match her new rose-gold locket and went down to join her aunt.

She found her on the back terrace, sitting at the table on which were a pitcher of sweet tea and two glasses. They talked about the plans she'd made with Jane and the upcoming dance. At 6:30 p.m., Marie came out with their dinner of rosemary-crusted lamb chops, mashed potatoes, and an assortment of garden vegetables dripping in butter and garlic. Lola's mouth watered as she thanked Marie. They were told that a cherry pie was warming in the oven and that Marie would make blueberry muffins for breakfast tomorrow. She bid them goodnight and was off.

Lola and Phyllis ate in companionable silence for a little while until Phyllis asked about Simon's letter. Lola smiled as she recalled the words and shared with Phyllis that it was beautiful and that it touched her a lot. She wished she had known her father and hoped that he hadn't suffered too much in the end. Her mom had never told her he was sick, only that he had left. And since it always made her mom sad to talk about it, she never asked her most pressing questions: Did her mom know he was sick? Did she think he had left for other reasons? That he didn't love her anymore? *Maybe Phyllis could answer some of these*, she thought. When Lola asked her, she responded that her mother knew about the illness and probably said he left because it was easier for a small child to understand. Phyllis surmised that she most likely meant to tell Lola when she got older, and then she got sick too. It was just so sad...

Phyllis said she would show her pictures of her father growing up, and in his later years, as well as any videos she might find. She told Lola that she could spend as much time as she wanted in her father's room. That nothing had been moved, only gently cleaned since he'd died thirteen years previously. At the time, it was too much to bear for her to go in there or try to sort anything out. But eventually, she just left things as they were, thinking Lola might want to see his room as it was when he lived in it. Lola was grateful and would indeed visit again, even if only to check out the Family Bible.

After they'd had their pie and coffee, Phyllis said she needed to return a few calls and suggested they meet upstairs in thirty minutes to resume the tour of the house.

CHAPTER 13
UPSTAIRS

THE ROOM next to Simon's was Phyllis.' Her room was South-facing, and her tower was in the Southwest corner, which meant she got the sun from midday to sunset. Phyllis told her that when she was a teenager, she thought it was perfect as she never had the morning sun to wake her. Now she had the run of the house; if she wanted to do Sun Salutations, she could follow the sun!

Her room was all in blues. From aqua to robin's egg, with teal and midnight blue. It was an eclectic mix of artifacts, souvenirs, books, and throw pillows. It was like walking into another time, another place. There was a certain order to this chaos, a logic to the madness. One thing was sure, Phyllis wasn't a neat freak!

In one of the corners, there was a hammock suspended between huge potted palms. At the foot of her bed, instead of the usual Hope chest, Phyllis had a treasure chest, straight out of a pirate movie. It was unreal.

Despite there being a walk-in closet and large en-suite to change in, Phyllis had a screen, and she actually used it as Lola could see this morning's clothing hanging precariously over one of the sides. Instead of the staid armchairs in front of the fireplace, there was a tipi tied to the ceiling, obviously to maintain its shape. Lola peered into it and saw that it was a cozy reading nook with stacks and stacks of books.

"Phyllis! What is this? Did you run away from the circus or something? Do you have a twin I don't know about?" asked Lola in disbelief.

"Oh, darling, aren't you funny!" Phyllis replied. "No, none of those things. It's just I lived such a sheltered existence in my youth, and to some extent, I still do, that the only way to travel the world was through books, travel conferences, and souvenirs from family and friends. It seems most people would remember I liked the color blue and that I was interested in everything. This is the collection of those interests gone wild! You may not know this, but you and I share a birthday. I'll turn forty-six when you turn sixteen. Isn't it extraordinary?" asked Phyllis.

"Wow, we should have a big party when Jane comes!" suggested Lola.

"I usually prefer small, intimate dinner parties. But this occasion needs to be done in high style. Yes, let's have a party! That way, you young people can continue with your festivities after us old dodgers have finished with our port," quipped Phyllis.

"You're not old, but I understand what you mean. It sounds great to me, but only if you are not the one to cook and serve it. Do you think we could ask Marie?" asked Lola.

"Yes, Marie comes in with her sisters when we have events so that she's not overwhelmed. Just let me know what you'd like to eat, and we'll arrange it. We'll wait until after the dance to send out invitations in case you want to invite some of the people you meet there," suggested Phyllis.

"Right, good idea," responded Lola.

"We can have a planning session later in the week. For now, let's continue the tour!"

On the second floor, only two rooms remained. The one on the Northwest corner next to Simon's and the one on the Southwest corner next to Phyllis.' These rooms were the same width as the nursery and had neither a tower nor a fireplace. Both had en-suites and were roughly the same size as the guest room. Phyllis said these were meant for her children, for a live-in governess, or as additional guest rooms, as required. Though they were tastefully decorated, there was nothing exceptional about them. Lola did a circular turn in the hallway and noticed two extra doors beside Simon and Phyllis' rooms, and Lola asked Phyllis about them.

"The door next to my room leads to the attic on the third floor, which we'll visit tomorrow. The door next to Simon's room is simply a linen closet. I don't have the key on me, but I'll show you when we visit the third floor," said Phyllis.

"Okay, sounds good. Are you going down to the library?"

"Not tonight. I think I'll turn in early. All that socializing today has worn me out! But you go ahead if you like."

"No, I think I'll call Jane back. There is so much more to tell her!"

"Have fun!"

"Thanks. I'll try to get up earlier and join you for yoga if you don't mind."

"That's no problem. I usually start at around 8 a.m."

"In the gazebo?"

"Yes, unless it's raining, then I'll be in the dance studio."

"Perfect. Goodnight, Phyllis!"

"Good night, Lola. Sleep well!"

Lola got back to her room and chatted for about an hour with Jane. Then she brushed her teeth, set the alarm, and sank into the plush covers, intent on a good night's sleep.

CHAPTER 14
YOGA

WHEN LOLA WOKE the next morning, she felt restless, like she was forgetting something important. And no matter how much she thought about it, she couldn't remember what she had dreamed about. No matter, she had no time to dwell on it as it was almost 8 a.m. She must have hit snooze a few times. She figured her PJs were appropriate yoga attire; she brushed her teeth and hair and, noticing the rain, headed next door to the gym. *Talk about a short commute.*

Phyllis was still meditating when she opened the door; she got a towel and a bottle of water and waited just outside the door until she was done. There was a chime, and the music stopped. Phyllis stretched her arms in the air and circled them back to her heart, and whispered, "Namaste" with a bow. Then she rose, saw Lola by the door, and gestured for her to enter.

"Good morning, darling. Did you sleep well?" she asked.

"I don't know. I woke up feeling restless, but I'm not tired or anything. Maybe all the changes are catching up with me. Or it's just new life jitters."

"A little yoga will do wonders!"

She took Lola through a few standing poses, then some sitting and floor ones, and finally some that were lying down and were meant to be relaxing. Lola felt relaxed yet energized. She liked yoga!

"May I join you every day? I mean, when I can wake up on time." Lola grinned, knowing she wasn't very good at getting up early.

"Yes, that would be lovely. Next time will be easier because you know the names of the poses."

"I hope I remember them! I liked how you told me when to breathe in and when to breathe out. It was super helpful," said Lola.

"My pleasure, dear. That was my favorite part too! If you can bear to wake a little earlier, I can show you how to meditate. I usually meditate for fifteen to twenty minutes. If you come at 7:30, I can explain a few things, and we'll go from there," suggested Phyllis.

"Yeah, sure. I read that meditation is not only good for relaxing, but it makes you healthier and smarter. I'm in!" Lola clapped her hands and did a little happy dance.

"Great," said Phyllis laughing. "I'm going to shower and change. Meet you in the sunroom at 10 a.m.?"

"Perfect!"

They both headed back to their rooms to shower and change. Since she was going to work after lunch and wouldn't feel like changing, Lola chose jeans, a t-shirt, and her red Chucks. She added a hoodie in case it was cold in the grocery store.

Realizing she had some free time, Lola decided to go set up the computer in her alcove and check her email. It was quick business, as there weren't that many. Sitting in the comfy swivel chair, Lola took inventory of the contents of the various cubby holes and drawers. There were the usual stationary articles, but a few items caught her fancy. The first was a stack of leather-bound journals in various pastel colors. The covers were buttery soft. They were unlined and held about one hundred pages of thick, porous, yellowish paper with scalloped edges. Upon closer inspection, Lola noticed the pages were, in fact, stitched, not glued, and there was a tasseled page keeper in the center. Lola was itching to write her thoughts into one of these!

The next items of interest were a quill and ink, perfectly suited to the journals. She'd never written with a quill and thought she might practice on plain paper to try her hand. She found some and thought for a moment what she might write. She decided to write out a list of all the things she was grateful for. There seemed to be many since she'd moved here: her aunt, the house, her first job, new friends in Bonnie and Jackson. Jackson.

She'd never fancied a boy before. And she'd never had such easy conversations with anyone but Jane. It was an odd combination. Mind you, she'd only spent a little time with him so far, but somehow, he felt......familiar. Like she'd known him forever. It was just unnerving to Lola how attractive he was. And he was very nice to her. It made her feel like he might be into her. But she was getting ahead of herself. She was probably reading way too much into it. Besides, Phyllis had probably asked him to be extra nice to her because she was new in town and didn't know anybody. Also, he was nineteen. Surely a boy that handsome, funny, and smart had his pick of girls who were way more sophisticated than Lola. Nonetheless, she was grateful for his easy companionship. It would have been awful to dislike each other and live in such close proximity.

Lola's stomach grumbled, and that prompted her to check the time. Time for breakfast!

CHAPTER 15
BREAKFAST

SHE WAS HALFWAY down the stairs when she smelled the blueberry muffins. That's when she knew she was in heaven. She was picturing fresh, creamy butter, melting on each half, and steamy coffee with cream and sugar, just itching for a muffin to be dunked into it. This is how the other half lived, she thought. No wonder they were cheerful! Who wouldn't be in a good mood when they did yoga upon waking and had fresh-out-of-the-oven muffins and piping hot, freshly ground coffee to start their day? Oh, and freshly squeezed orange juice, fresh, ready-to-eat fruit, homemade bread, and preserves, of course! She bet even the bacon was fresh. There must be a pork farm around here somewhere. Was that the right term? She'd have to look it up.

A deep voice brought her out of her thoughts. "Are you going to eat breakfast or just stand there and smell it from the door with a goofy grin on your face?" teased Jackson from the table.

Lola's eyes snapped open upon hearing Jackson's voice. He kept popping up when she wasn't expecting him. This would take some getting used to. "I was appreciating the food before I have it. It smells delicious!" Lola responded.

What was Jackson doing here? There was no point in being embarrassed now; she walked in and went to the sideboard to get coffee and juice. She was debating where to sit, as Jackson was sitting where she sat yesterday. She wanted to be able to look out at the grounds, but she felt foolish sitting right next to him. Facing him would have her facing the sideboard.

As if reading her mind, Jackson said, "Take Phyllis' spot. She went to eat on the porch. I prefer to eat here. It's closer to the food."

Lola looked unsure and replied, "Maybe I should go join Phyllis. She said to meet her here at 10 a.m."

Jackson shrugged his shoulders and said, "She had a book with her and didn't seem like she wanted company."

Lola set her drinks down and went to load up her plate. "That settles it, then. Do you eat here every morning? I didn't see you yesterday."

"I do, but I'm usually done by 8:30. I'm running late today. A few unexpected chores kept me up late last night, and I overslept this morning," he explained.

Lola came back to the table, sat down, and replied, "How mysterious! What chores?"

"The grounds are quite extensive, and it's difficult to keep an eye on all the borders. We have perimeter sensors that relay information to a console I have set up on my computer. Three of them were set off last night; I had to investigate."

Lola broke off a piece of the muffin top, slathered it with butter, and stuffed it in her mouth. She moaned in delight, and Jackson chuckled. When she was finished chewing, she commented, "Wow, that's pretty sophisticated! Is this a high crime area?"

"Not really, but we don't like surprise visitors getting too near the house. Last night, those visitors were of the animal variety," said Jackson.

Lola kept eating, and this time her mouth was still full when she asked, "Like a bear?"

Jackson was tucking into eggs and bacon and shook his head before replying, "Deer and rabbits, mostly. I'm going to do a perimeter walk this morning to ensure all the sensors are working correctly and that there are no animals stuck in the metal link fence. Would you like to come with me? We could tour the grounds while we're at it," he offered.

"Sure, sounds like a fun way to walk off this breakfast," replied Lola.

"You're too skinny as it is. Good, southern cooking will fatten you up a bit," stated Jackson.

Lola stopped chewing and stared at him. When she didn't reply, he added, "You could also stand to get some sun; you've got that pasty city-girl look, with shadows under your eyes."

Lola glared at him and said, "Wow, you really know how to make a girl feel pretty."

Jackson put down his utensils and put his hands up in surrender. "It's not an insult, don't get your panties in a knot. I'm just saying you'll be even more attractive after a few days of southern living."

"Fair point," she said dubiously.

"I suggest you borrow Phyllis' boots from the mudroom, so you don't get those Chucks dirty, and grab a slicker too. It looks like it'll be raining all day today."

"Remember I have to work at 1 p.m.," said Lola.

"Don't worry, we'll be back in time for lunch and your first driving lesson!" exclaimed Jackson.

Lola was stuffed. She sat back in her chair and polished off her coffee. "Driving, already?"

"We'll take it slow, just the basics. Now come on, we've got a long walk ahead of us."

CHAPTER 16

ESTATE

BEFORE LEAVING, Lola stopped in to see Phyllis on the porch to let her know where she was going. But Phyllis wasn't there, so she left a note with Marie in the kitchen.

They started with the *backyard*, which in addition to the back terrace and gazebo Lola had seen, also included a fenced-in pool and pool house, stables with two horses, and a large paddock. There was also a small cottage, which Lola figured they had rebuilt after the fire that killed Jackson's parents. She assumed he didn't want to live there due to the memories, even if the house was new. It would serve for the next caretakers but could probably be used to accommodate additional guests or even be rented out to a trusted friend of the family.

Beyond these buildings, the Estate was mostly forest. But Lola soon saw there were well-defined trails for walking and asked how big the Estate was. Jackson told her it was forty-five acres. Lola had no idea what that meant, but he seemed quite proud of it, so it must be big. She made an impressed face and mouthed *wow*. Jackson seemed pleased.

They walked for about half a mile to the back fence. It looked like a regular 6-foot black chain-link fence with privacy strips. However, Jackson showed her the sensors, spaced every 100 meters, which added an extra *fence* made of infrared beams. Lola was a bit lost. It sounded like something out of a Mission Impossible movie.

"Photoelectric beam sensors are usually made up of a transmitter and a receiver. Both parts have an optical lens to help the infrared travel at a ,long-range. When the photoelectric beam sensors work, the transmitter is continuously emitting an infrared beam that travels a long distance to reach the receiver. This forms an invisible fence between transmitter and receiver so that it can be used to detect moving objects, like animals or trespassers. Imagine if we stood to face each other with red flashlights in the dark 100 meters from one another. That's what it looks like," explained Jackson.

"Got it. Like that movie where the spy has to go over and under the red beams without tripping them, but outside instead of in a museum," countered Lola.

"Exactly! Plus, it's all connected to my computer, but it also connects to an app on my phone. Even when I'm away from the estate, I can still keep tabs on it. We have a similar system installed in the house. But only on the doors and windows, so don't worry about tripping them accidentally," said Jackson.

They walked the perimeter counterclockwise, checking the fence for trapped animals and the sensors for obstacles like branches or vines. They talked as they walked, and Lola told him about deciding to be homeschooled for her senior year, and he agreed it was a good idea. But he still thought she should make an effort to integrate socially through parties, dances, and committees. If she decided to take distance college classes later, he told her that he'd join her, and they could keep each other accountable. Even if they didn't study the same field, they could still provide moral support and help each other prepare for exams and such. Lola thought that was a terrific idea. She was about to say it would be like having a brother, but it somehow didn't feel right.

The truth was, she liked Jackson. And though she didn't know him well, they would be spending an awful lot of time together from now on, like siblings. But then again, there was that whole thing that their parents thought they might make a good match, and it hung in the air between them. She was the heir to the Estate. He was more than the manager and caretaker. He obviously cared about it a lot. She thought he deserved it more than she did, and it would make sense for them to team up. But sense and feelings were two different things. No one said anything about forced marriage, thank the lord! She was free to marry, or not marry, whoever she wanted. She could live, or not live, in the house until her aunt died. Phyllis was in excellent health; she had at least another thirty years in her. By then, Lola would be her age! Surely at that stage, she would be ready for lunches, fundraisers, and Estate management.

"Lola!" Jackson cried out.

"What?"

"You're about to walk right into a tree! Snap out of it!" said Jackson as he shook her arm gently.

"Oh, thanks. I guess my thoughts ran away with me. Sorry. Did you say anything else?" asked Lola sheepishly.

"I asked if you had any idea what you wanted to study in college," repeated Jackson.

Lola ran her hands through her hair and hoped he didn't think she was a total moron. "I have no idea. My interests have always revolved around reading, maybe English Literature. I kind of figured I'd choose something practical during my senior year, like teaching. But now, knowing I'm expected to live here and have kids and that I don't need, nor am I encouraged to earn a wage, I have more choices. Including not going to college or even studying art to see if I have any of my dad's talent," said Lola.

As they walked and talked, Jackson checked the perimeter and periodically input something on his phone. "Maybe you're a writer! Or you could be an editor! The sky's the limit!" exclaimed Jackson.

"Who knows," Lola said, a thoughtful expression on her face. "That's sort of what I was thinking about. The future. It's a lot to take in, and it's not at all what I thought my future would look like," she said with emphasis.

"What do you expect would have happened if your mom hadn't

died?" asked Jackson. Then he stopped walking and touched Lola's arm lightly. "I'm sorry, Lola, that's insensitive," he apologized.

"No, it's a fair question. And since you've been through it, you're allowed to ask," replied Lola putting her hand on his. But she quickly dropped her hand and started walking again as she thought of her answer. "I figured I'd have finished high school, got a teaching degree at a community college, got a job, met a guy, taken out a mortgage, had some kids. You know, the usual," she stated plainly.

"Actually, you might have ended up here anyway. Once you turned eighteen, you would have gotten a letter from the lawyers. Which I assume would be sufficient to at least get you curious enough to come to meet your aunt and see where your father had grown up. Then, we'd be in this same spot! Only you would have a choice as to whether you stayed or not because you'd be old enough to live on your own and make your own decisions. You can't escape your fate," said Jackson.

"I hadn't thought about it that way. I don't like feeling like I'm not in control of my own destiny. It's depressing. I know I've just been showered with riches, and I have a home and a family. It could have been much worse, and I shouldn't complain. But still......" she trailed off.

Jackson nodded in agreement but made no comment. They kept walking, and he kept checking on the fence. They had circled back to the mid-point path and came upon a bench. Though it was drizzling by then, they decided to sit for a while. They had slickers, and the weather was warm.

"What about you?" Lola tried to redirect the conversation around Jackson. "What do you want to study in college?"

"I had planned on going to college and getting an MBA, probably at John Madison, then come back here and to do this exact same job, only later and better. You and I would have met two years later, arriving back here at about the same time. Phyllis and my parents would have introduced us with high hopes of us getting together. I might have met someone at college, but it probably wouldn't have worked out. As I said, you can't escape your fate," he said simply.

"I'd like to say this is a load of crap, but I feel like you're right. My mom always said, 'There's no such thing as fate. Life is what you make of it.' She was quite insistent about it, like she had a point to prove. But if you're right, that means horrible things had to happen to get us here, together," said Lola.

"Not exactly. It just means our parents made choices that had deadly consequences."

Lola gasped and said, "What are you saying?"

"Your parents were meant to live in this house and have two kids like everybody else before them. Why did they move back to Baltimore?" asked Jackson.

"Good question. You're saying they were punished for not following the rules. That's insane!" Lola said, shaking her head.

"Not punished, per se. But their choices changed the order of things, and the Universe sometimes has a harsh way of self-correcting. There is more at play than you realize," said Jackson gravely.

"Obviously! It sounds like you're talking about supernatural occurrences. What about your parents. Why did they die?" asked Lola.

"I've been wrestling with that one," Jackson conceded. "I wasn't here. I don't know exactly what happened before the fire. Horace's descendants were fated to be here. Maybe my parents wanted me to change things, to get our name back as a prominent, wealthy family? After college, they might have wanted me to branch out on my own instead of being *indentured* to the Evers. Sort of like becoming the king of my own castle instead of becoming a king by marrying the queen of this one. But you see, I've always loved it here. It was my home. I care deeply about Phyllis as if she was my own aunt. I care about the Estate, about seeing it prosper, even if it's not mine. I don't have personal ambitions or goals. All of my goals are for the Estate. I feel flaky saying it like that, as though I've been brainwashed or under a spell. But it's the truth," he said, looking down at his hands as though avoiding her gaze.

This was getting intense. She only met this boy a few days ago. She had a whole new life, with a whole new set of life goals she knew nothing about. Panic was starting to creep into her voice as she exclaimed, "Doesn't it freak you out that your whole life was decided for you?" Lola ventured, "That your life partner is probably a 15-year-old girl you'd never seen before two days ago?"

Jackson could obviously hear the shriek in her voice, knew it was rising panic, and hoped his answer would be a soothing one. "It should, but it doesn't," he replied. He looked up and into her eyes as he said, "I like my life. And I like you, Lola."

As he talked, he was inching closer to her, but Lola hadn't noticed. She was too caught up with her freak-out. He took her hands and kept staring into her eyes for a moment. Now she was paying attention! Her heart started beating really fast, and she blushed. She could tell she was about to start babbling like an idiot, but then he kissed her. It was a soft kiss, closed mouth, her first. It felt like the world started spinning. She clutched his hands, closed her eyes, and kissed him back. It was wonderful. The rain stopped, the sun came out, the birds started chirping. Time stood still. She was smiling when Jackson pulled back. But when she opened her eyes, she saw it was still raining lightly, and nothing had changed. She had changed! She wanted more of this! She leaned in, hoping to kiss him again, but Jackson leaned back on the bench, smiled, and rose. "I think that's enough excitement for today!" he said gently and motioned towards the path.

It was almost time for lunch, so they headed back in silence. Lola kept watching Jackson for any sign that the kiss had been a mistake. But he had a relaxed smile on his face like all was right with the world. Lola, on the other hand, was a nervous wreck. *What does it mean? Did fate make us kiss? Are we sincerely attracted to each other? Does he like me? Why?* There was nothing special about her. She was quite ordinary. And anything exceptional about it had happened in the last two days. What could a 19-year-old boy see in an almost 16-year-old girl?

Lola told herself to stop overthinking this. *It was a kiss. It was nice. Get over it!*

As though sensing her insecurity, he took her hand, and they held hands all the way back to the house. From the window, Phyllis smiled at them though they did not see her. At lunch, they both acted like everything was normal and didn't realize how much Phyllis was biting her tongue. Soon it was time to leave for Lola's first day at work.

CHAPTER 17
WORK

BEFORE THEY LEFT, Jackson had her walk around the car and name basic car parts, then he did the same inside the car. As he drove, he kept a running monologue of the steps he was taking, what he was doing, and what he was keeping an eye on. That was her first driving lesson as an active observer. It was hard to stay focused. To pay attention, she had to look at him. But the more she looked at him, the more she fell for him. All she could think about was that kiss and when they could have another. Were they dating now? Damn, she wished she had paid more attention to Jane when she talked about boys and dating. She should know this stuff, right?

"Are you even listening to me?" Jackson's words cut into Lola's thoughts.

"Yes, yes, you said I should always yield to pedestrians, even if there isn't a crosswalk and even if it doesn't say so in the driver's manual because this is the South and we're not heathens," repeated Lola.

"Okay, just checking. You had that goofy smile on your face again," said Jackson with a smile.

Lola blushed and was about to tell him she'd never been kissed before and that it was a major deal for her, but how lame would that sound to a 19-year-old boy? A man, really. Oh god, she thought, Jackson has probably had sex. She wasn't ready for sex. She was freaking out about holding hands and kissing a boy.

"Breathe, Lola, breathe!" Jackson said. "I don't know what you're panicking about now, but everything is going to be okay. We're here. I'll be back at 5 p.m. to pick you up. Have fun!" he said, punching her arm lightly.

"Thanks!" Lola said, her heart racing.

She got out of the car and wondered how he could tell what she was thinking. Was he a mind-reader? She really hoped he wasn't. Otherwise, she would die of humiliation. She walked into the Food Lion and went directly to find Mr. Xavier. When she called him that, he said his name was Xavier Morton but that she should call him Xavier like everyone else. He gave her a tour of the grocery store and a list of tasks. The first task was to open shipment boxes, check the accuracy of the contents, label them, and then put the items on the shelves. Labeling was the best part! Then, she was to go through an inventory list in the stock room.

She was engrossed in this task when Xavier came to tell her Jackson was there to pick her up.

"Already?" she asked, astonished.

"It's 5 o'clock!" he replied.

"Oh, time flies when you're having fun!" said Lola.

"So, you enjoyed yourself?" he asked.

"Yes, I did. See you tomorrow?" she asked hopefully.

"Of course. We have a deal until Friday," said Xavier with a nod.

"Fantastic, thanks, Mister, I mean, Xavier," replied Lola with a grin.

"See you tomorrow, Lola!" he said and waved goodbye.

She got in the car and told Jackson all about her first day at work. It was too cool! And she must have done a good job if Xavier was letting her come back the next day. Regardless of their agreement, if she had been awful, she doubted he would let her return, especially now that she knew everyone else knew she didn't need the money. I mean, sure, they said the house and the money were hers. And her aunt had bought her a bunch of clothes. But it's not like anybody had given her any cash or the keys to the safe deposit box, or even to the house now that she thought about it. If she wanted to buy a pack of gum, she would need some money, and she didn't have that much saved up.

Once he had her attention again, Jackson resumed his driving instructor persona. He was taking this seriously! Maybe he was already sick of driving her around. He was good at it. Patient, precise, always explaining why things were done the way they were. Besides, she could watch the way his mouth formed words all day.

His voice crashed into her dreaming. "Lola!" he said sternly.

"What?!!?" she said guiltily. If he could read her mind, she was in BIG trouble.

"I asked if you wanted to visit the garage and my apartment tomorrow morning."

"Yes, of course! Unless Phyllis has other plans for me. It's the only place I haven't seen yet besides the third floor of the house."

"Do you have a cell phone?" Jackson asked.

"Um, no," said Lola, the blush on her cheeks growing redder. "It was canceled with all our other accounts. But I have an iPad," she offered.

"That's okay for now; the Wi-Fi range extends to most of the Estate. Do you have a Gmail account?" he inquired.

"Yes, it's lola4evers, all lowercase and with a number, not a word."

"Clever. Mine is dixon_jackson, also lowercase."

"How very boring, yet professional of you," quipped Lola.

"I'll check in with you tonight to confirm after you've had time to review your schedule with Phyllis," promised Jackson.

"Sounds great. Thanks for the ride!" Lola said, unbuckling her seatbelt.

"Anytime, Lola. Soon enough, you'll be driving yourself," he added.

He dropped her off at the front entrance and made his way back to the garage.

CHAPTER 18
ATTORNEY

AFTER SHE ARRIVED BACK, Lola got ready for dinner and met her aunt promptly at 6 p.m. in the sitting room off the dining room. They had a guest! The tall man, dressed like an English lord in a three-piece suit and sporting a lavaliere no less, must have been at least 100 years old. He sat, ramrod straight, like a former army general, and had the most piercing blue eyes that bore right into Lola when he set them upon her.

"Darling! Please come and meet our very important guest. This is Mr. Edward J. Radcliff, III, our attorney. Edward, this is Lola, my niece and heir to the throne as it were," said Phyllis with a flourish.

"Indeed, Ms. Evers, it is a pleasure meeting you at last!" he said, his manner as impeccable as his attire.

"It's a pleasure meeting you, Mr. Edward." Lola almost felt the need to curtsey.

"Oh, do call me Edward. I won't feel quite so ancient," replied the attorney.

"Yes, of course, sir," said Lola demurely.

"Come, sit, and tell me a little about yourself. We had only the most basic information from your mother over the years. Mostly that you were healthy and doing well in school. Not a word about how you turned into such a lovely young lady!" he said with a wink.

Lola blushed and tried to be eloquent and poised in her response. There wasn't much to tell. But she rattled off her interests and a few accomplishments. The attorney smiled as he listened, nodding appreciatively as though she was saying she had won a Nobel prize in astrophysics.

"And how about you, Edward? Have you been working with the Evers family for a long time?" Lola inquired politely.

"Goodness, yes! It seems like it's been forever. In a way, it has. My ancestor John T. Radcliff was one of the first to settle here in 1620. He was a barrister and counseled the Evers of his time. It's been that way for generations now," he explained.

"So, you know all of our secrets and where all the bodies are buried, then?" Lola joked.

His face fell, and Lola immediately regretted her attempt at humor. Everyone was very serious. But after a minute or so, Edward started laughing and slapping his thigh.

"She's a funny one! How refreshing you are, Ms. Evers," he said with genuine mirth.

"Please, if I'm to call you Edward, you must call me Lola!" replied Lola shyly.

"And so, I shall!" said the attorney.

Marie came in just then and told them dinner was ready. They moved to the dining room, and Edward told her about the Estate, the family through the ages, and about her responsibilities as heir. It turned out she didn't own the house. No single Evers owned anything. There was a trust, and the heir was the custodian, or keeper, of the Trust. Each Evers family member received a part of the trust in three separate payouts, just as she had described to Jane.

The heir also received part of the trust in three shares but timed differently than the other family members: one when they turn eighteen, the second when they get married, and the third upon the birth of their firstborn. The heir ensured that the Trust prospered for future generations, that the Estate was well maintained and renovated or updated as required, that the Evers family was well represented in the community, and, through marriage and children, ensured the perpetuation of the Evers line.

The heir is always the eldest of the children. Should the heir not have children of their own for whatever reason, then the heir would be their sibling's children. In this case, since only Simon had children, there could only be one heir: Lola. In addition to these responsibilities, the heir was also keeper to the Evers Archives—apparently, a large book containing sensitive family information. Whatever that meant.

After dinner, they retired to the library to sign some papers. Mainly attesting that Lola was the heir but that Phyllis would act as her guardian and continue as temporary custodian of the Estate until she reached eighteen years of age. She was given a set of keys to the mansion and all outbuildings, a checkbook, an ATM card, a credit card, a new cell phone, and a list of calendar events she was required to attend in the coming year. Until her eighteenth birthday, she would get a monthly allowance to spend at her discretion. This ungodly amount, one thousand dollars per month, would be deposited into her bank account automatically. Lola was shell-shocked.

"Do you have any questions, Lola?" Edward enquired.

"Not at present, Edward, but I'm sure I'll have plenty once this all sinks in!" responded Lola, as though from very far away.

"I know it's a lot to take in," he responded. "Had you grown up here, you would have been prepared incrementally for the task at hand. As it stands, you have two years to become a respected member of society and learn the ropes from Phyllis. That's why homeschooling is the best option for someone in your position because you'll need time to learn a few extra skills befitting your status. Also, though young Jackson is doing a fine job learning as he goes and managing the assets, you will have to learn as well, since it is ultimately your responsibility. I believe you've been told he is a suitable match for you, but remember, choosing him for your mate is not mandatory, though it is highly recommended. Not only because of his intimate knowledge of the family's affairs but also because of his family's history. He also happens to be a fine young man and quite good-looking!" Edward said with a wink.

Edward started packing up his things. He explained that Phyllis also had much to impart in the coming months and would refer questions to Edward. She couldn't answer herself. They said goodnight and promised to keep in touch.

CHAPTER 19
GARAGE

LOLA WAS TOO KEYED up to sit with a book in the library after dinner. She excused herself and started dialing Jane on her new cell as she walked to her room. She quickly realized this might be too much for Jane to take in since Lola could barely believe it herself. She put away her cell phone and decided to mull this over some more. She was pacing her room when her iPad pinged. Jackson! She raced over to check her message.

dixon_jackson@gmail.com: Hey, Lola, are we on for tomorrow am?

lola4evers@gmail.com: Oh, I forgot to ask Phyllis. Gimme five.

Lola raced back down the stairs to ask her aunt about their morning plans. Phyllis responded that she was hoping to finish the tour of the third floor and show her the Archives. Lola said goodnight to Phyllis and left her in the library.

Without thinking, Lola walked to the mudroom, put on boots, grabbed a slicker, and headed towards the garage. One of the doors was open, and she could hear music playing. As she neared, she saw Jackson working on his truck. He was wearing faded, torn, blue jeans and an old gray ACDC t-shirt. He was bobbing his head and singing along to the song playing. She didn't know the band, but it was good. She knocked on the side door to announce herself, but he couldn't hear her; she got closer and yelled his name. Still nothing. She walked up to him and put a hand on his shoulder. He jumped, bumped his head on the hood of the car, and turned to her in surprise.

"I'm really sorry! I knocked and called your name, but the music was too loud," she said and giggled.

"What are you doing here?" he asked, slightly annoyed.

"You're busy. I'm sorry, I didn't think, I just came over," Lola stammered.

She turned to leave, but he grabbed her hand and brought her to face him.

"Is there a reason for this visit, or did you miss me already?" said Jackson with a smile.

Lola's heart was pounding. This was flirting, and she was obviously ill-equipped. All she could do was smile and say what she came to say, "Um, well, I went down to ask Phyllis. She said we'll be visiting the attic tomorrow and I don't want to miss that. I was going to go back up and write to you, but I figured this would be quicker, and besides, I need to talk to someone about all this. I was going to call Jane, my best friend back home, but there's no way she could relate to all this. And, well, my feet brought me here before I gave it any thought. And now I've invaded your privacy—"

He placed a finger on her lips to silence her and told her to slow down and take a breath. She did, and it calmed her a bit. Then she showed him the cell phone, keys, and checkbook she was still holding in her hands.

"They gave me all this stuff! It's real now!" she exclaimed.

"Okay. What do we have here?" he asked gently, leading her to some stacks of tires they could sit on.

"This is the checkbook and ATM card for my account. I get an allowance every month until I'm eighteen. It's so huge they thought I might need a checkbook! This is the credit card I use. A credit card? I thought you had to be over eighteen to have a credit card!" exclaimed Lola.

"Well, it's a family card with your name on it. You're not responsible for paying the balance every month. It's what they give students for monthly expenses, or sometimes it's given to a spouse who doesn't work and won't qualify for one on their own," said Jackson matter-of-factly.

"Oh, okay. Thanks for the info. I know nothing! I still can't believe they would hand over an Estate to a teenager!" wailed Lola.

"Well, they haven't YET. They've given you the keys to your home and money for spending like they would any other minor living in the house. When you turn eighteen, THAT's when the real responsibilities start. But don't worry, I'll be here to help," he said soothingly.

As if hoping to steer them to a safer topic, Jackson took her through the garage. It was a four-car garage. There was his pick-up that he was working on, the fancy car they had taken when driving Phyllis to her appointments, a small red sports car, and the last door led to a tractor. Lola didn't know anything about cars. Her mom had an old, beat-up Honda. She approached each car and peered inside. It was all terribly overwhelming.

Assuming to sense her unease, Jackson piped up, "You don't know anything about cars, right?"

"I know that one—John Deere!" Lola teased.

"Funny! The black car is a Bentley. It's the family car. It's usually driven by a chauffeur, which would be me at present, to transport the Evers to functions. The red car is a Maserati. It was your dad's, but it's still in excellent condition. It's yours now, but I won't let you drive it until you're good and ready. Not only is it super expensive, but it's also considered vintage now."

"I'm not going near that thing for a while, then!" declared Lola. "I don't want to be responsible for a collector's item!"

"Let's move on with the tour. That closet has various products and parts for car maintenance. Normally, when the house is full, there is a full-time chauffeur, and the apartment would be his. The cottage on the grounds is for the groundskeeper and housekeeper; they've always been a matched pair for as long as I can tell. Chauffeurs tend to be unattached due to having to drive at odd times like in the evening or for overnight trips. This door leads to the apartment, but there's another one outside with a separate driveway where my truck should be parked."

"Why did you take your truck to pick me up when I got here on Sunday if you had these other two to choose from?" asked Lola.

"I thought you'd have a ton of stuff, and the Bentley's trunk isn't that roomy."

"Oh, smart," Lola said.

It was getting late, and at Lola's yawn, Jackson walked her back to the house and went into the mudroom with her. She now had the opportunity to try her keys, and he showed her how to deactivate the alarm.

"It's pretty simple. This round plastic thing has a chip in it. You touch it to the sensor when you come in, and it recognizes you. If someone had the key but not the chip, a silent alarm would go off. You have thirty seconds to do it. When you've got your keys in your hand, you can just wave the lot at the sensor. The alarm kicks in at 10 p.m. every night and stays on until 7 a.m. when Marie comes in. She has a key, but no chip, so she can't come and go outside those hours. When the family is away from the house, the alarm is always on."

Lola looked impressed. "The security here is really sophisticated."

"It's the same for the outbuildings, the garage, the cottage, and my apartment. Anyway, it's late. We should both get some sleep," said Jackson as he gave her a chaste kiss on the forehead and went back to his apartment.

CHAPTER 20
SAD

LOLA OPENED her eyes to a sunny day and a happy heart. What a day! Her first driving lesson—even though she didn't actually drive—her first job, her first checkbook, and a credit card. It was unreal. She felt like jumping up and down. She should do just that! She got up on her bed and started jumping and squealing like she was at a 6-year-old's birthday party. She was the luckiest girl in the world. Then she felt guilty for being happy. Her mom died less than three months ago. She should be sad, right? This was confusing. Now she felt like crying and realized tears were running down her cheeks. She plopped back down on her bed and stared at the ceiling.

There was a knock on the door, and she yelled, "Come in!" Whether or not the knocker heard her, they entered, and she heard her aunt ask if she was decent. She said she was and to come on into the bedroom. Her aunt had a tray laden with breakfast items.

"When I didn't see you at yoga or breakfast, I thought you might be ill. Then as I was coming up the stairs, I heard a yelp coming from your room. Is everything alright, darling?"

"Oh my God, I'm so embarrassed! I should confess, I was jumping on my bed. What time is it?"

"It's 10 a.m. But you look like you've been crying?" Phyllis asked worriedly.

"Welcome to the joys of being a teenager," sniffed Lola.

"How can I help? I've brought you some breakfast. Want to chat over coffee and muffins?"

"Yes, please!"

Lola got to try her little bistro table and chairs. Imagine having a tray brought to her room. If she'd been sick, she might have had breakfast in bed!

Phyllis poured them each a cup and waited for Lola to open up about what was bothering her.

"Have you ever been happy and sad at the same time?" Lola started.

"Yes, I have," Phyllis responded. "It seems paradoxical to have two contradicting emotions at the same time, but we humans are a complex bunch."

"Tell me about it! I was so happy about yesterday. There were so many firsts for me. It was exciting! Like a dream come true. Then I felt guilty for being happy when my mom just died."

"I know how you feel," Phyllis continued. "When Simon died, I was sad that he was gone, angry that he left me here all alone, relieved that I no longer had to care for him, and guilty for being angry and relieved! On days when I felt happy, I felt guilty about that too. I was a mess!" Phyllis took a sip of coffee, seeming nonplussed despite the admission.

"Wow, that's a lot to deal with. I didn't realize you were the one who took care of him. I figured he was at the hospital." Lola picked at her muffin, waiting for her to continue.

"He wanted to stay home, and we did have a nurse stay overnight to provide medical care, bathe and dress him. But I stayed with him during the day, fed him, took him to the bathroom. I read him a lot, and in the end, he slept a lot and we listened to a lot of music. He didn't like the silence." Phyllis turned and looked out the window as she said that last part. She seemed miles away like she was reliving those last days with her brother.

The sadness crept into Lola's voice. "I'm sorry you had to go through that. I understand why he left. It would have been too much for my mom." Lola took a large gulp of her coffee, hoping it would steady her.

"He loved her very much. But I was grateful that he came back to stay here before he died. I missed him terribly while he was away. We'd never been separated before he left with your mom."

"Wow, I never thought of that." Lola looked thoughtful. "Didn't he go away to school like Jackson? Isn't that how he met my mom?"

"No, he was homeschooled with me. But sometimes, he attended lectures he was interested in at various universities. I believe your parents met at a party Simon was invited to after a lecture. Since he was staying overnight and he had nothing better to do, he decided to go to the party just for the experience. You see, neither of us had ever been to a college party. From what he told me, it was a memorable one!"

"How so?" asked Lola quizzically.

Phyllis grabbed the coffee pot and refilled their cups before she continued.

"He said it was just like in the movies. Total mayhem. Kegs everywhere, half-naked girls standing around drinking, fully clothed people in the pool, and couples making out all over the place."

Lola was reaching for some grapes when her eyes widened, and her jaw dropped. "What was my mom doing at a party like THAT?"

Phyllis chuckled at that. "She was with Simone, and believe me, she was the life of the party. When Simon first saw her, she was upside down chugging a beer through a tube, with over fifty people cheering her on."

"Shut. The. Front. Door. My mother? Elaine Harris?" said Lola, shocked.

"Yes! She was apparently quite the party animal before she met Simon. It's one of the things that drew him to her. He was stuck in his head, too serious. It's an odd trait from an artist. But he was always more of a misunderstood artist than an eccentric one. Anyway, things got hot and heavy that night, and he took her back to his hotel. The next day, they went to the town hall and got married. He came home, packed a few things, went back to Baltimore, and moved in with your mom. We all thought it was a phase and that he'd come to his senses. Sorry, but it's the truth. They were quite different and from such different backgrounds. And of course, she wasn't on the approved list of brides my parents had been meticulously drawing up for years."

"About that. The list of approved matches. Do I have one?" Lola asked wryly.

"Not yet, but I was hoping I'd start one as I got to know you. The eligible young men in the area will be at this year's social events. The ones on your social calendar. Why do you ask?"

"Jackson and I were talking. He suggested I ask for a list if I was feeling pressured to marry him specifically. I'd feel like I had choices."

"Of course, you have choices!" Phyllis exclaimed. "We're not going to pick someone for you and force you to marry them. That would be barbaric! I want you to be happy here. This is your home, and it will be the home of your husband, children, and grandchildren. Happy couples make happy kids and contribute to a healthy, wealthy, and happy future for everyone. Don't overthink this too much."

Lola nodded. "That's what Jackson said."

"Seems you and Jackson have been getting pretty close these last few days," Phyllis said with a wink.

"I've spent as much time with him as I have with you. He feels like family but more."

"More? Do tell!" said Phyllis, leaning in.

"Well, we kissed," said Lola shyly.

"Oh my! Was it your first?" Phyllis looked so happy. It was as though it had been her first kiss too.

"Yes!! It was amazing!"

"When did this happen?"

"He kissed me yesterday morning during our Estate walkthrough. Just a peck, really, though it blew my socks off!"

"That is something," Phyllis said, smiling. "And then?"

"Nothing since, last night after showing me how to use the keys and the key card, he kissed my forehead and said goodnight," said Lola with a sigh.

"What a gentleman! I got a little worried there for a minute! He is a bit older than you, you know," Phyllis said, relief on her face.

"I know! I bet he has all kinds of experience," said Lola, emphasizing the word experience and waving her eyebrows comically.

Phyllis laughed despite herself. "Not as much as you might expect for his age. He and I have had many heart-to-hearts. Since his mom wasn't available, I was the closest thing to a mom he had. Let's just say he was a late bloomer!" Phyllis winked. "Which is why I'm not all that worried that you two are spending so much time alone," she added.

"Oh, good. That makes me feel better. I had no idea what I was doing!" confessed Lola.

"Don't overthink that either. Do what comes naturally but still feels right. Don't rush into anything. You have plenty of time before you decide on a mate. Even if you wanted to get married before eighteen, I wouldn't give my consent. You need time to grow into yourself, see a bit more of the world, and have a taste of what is out there. Don't go giving your heart to the first boy who turns your head. It may be that you and Jackson end up together, but I agree that you should sample a few other selections on life's menu! Have a little fun!" said Phyllis with a nudge.

Lola laughed so hard she snorted. "Like my mom?" she asked.

Phyllis stopped laughing and replied, "Well, maybe not that much fun!" Then Phyllis stopped and looked up as an idea occurred to her. "Perhaps we should have a conversation about drinking responsibly and safe sex."

Lola rolled her eyes. "Don't worry, Phyllis, my mom may have had a misspent youth, but she was quite adamant that I not have any fun. We've had the drinking talk and the sex talk. She was planning on getting me a doctor's appointment for the pill when I turned sixteen......" Lola trailed off, looking a bit embarrassed.

Phyllis assured her she would make an appointment for her with her physician. It was a good idea to get a check-up anyhow. Then, she rang for Marie to come to take the tray and left Lola to get dressed so they could complete the tour of the house. They were to meet at the door to the third floor, with her new keys, in thirty minutes.

Lola checked her messages and was happy to see one from Jane and one from Jackson. She read Jane's first, out of loyalty. It was a short one, confirming her arrival on Thursday on the 5 p.m. bus. Perfect timing! She and Jackson could go pick her up after work, and she'd have time to shower and change before dinner. She replied that she was sooo looking forward to her visit and had a ton of new things to tell her.

Next, she read Jackson's message. He had sent it last night. A short message telling her to have sweet dreams. How sweet! She was about to close the iPad when another message from Jackson came in. He was asking what her new phone number was so he could text or call her. She had no idea! She went to get it and realized it was written on a sticker on the box. She quickly wrote him a thank you for last night's message, added her new cell phone number, and wrote that she'd see him after lunch for the drive into work.

She then got dressed, grabbed her keys, and went to meet her aunt.

CHAPTER 21
ATTIC

THEY MET in front of the door to the attic. Phyllis showed her which key to use, and the door was soon open. Ordinary wooden stairs led to the third floor, where another door waited, but no key was required. But before letting Lola open the door, Phyllis put her hand on Lola's hand to stop her.

"When coming to the attic, you should always close and lock the door at the bottom," she cautioned.

"Why? So, no one creeps in and startles me?" joked Lola.

"Not exactly, though that is a very good reason. First, if you can lock the door, it means you have the keys on you and will be able to open the next door. It's so you don't get locked in the stairwell."

"But Phyllis, this door has no lock," said Lola, bemused.

"Right, of course. There is no way of explaining this. It's best to show you."

Lola gave Phyllis a strange look. "You're giving me the creeps, Phyllis. What's in the attic?"

"I'm sorry, I don't mean to. I never expected to have to explain this to anyone. For most, this door leads to the attic where we store old furniture and knick-knacks." Phyllis opened the door, and they walked into a cluttered room full of antiques, portraits, and furniture, all covered with white sheets to protect against dust. It was unimpressive. Phyllis closed the door behind them, and Lola released the breath she was holding. It was just an attic.

"Now, this is where it gets interesting," said Phyllis with a gleam in her eye. Out of her pocket, she produced an ancient-looking key with a red tassel at the end. "This is an Evers key. It's a special key," explained Phyllis as she put it in the lock on the door leading back down to the second floor. She opened the door to show Lola that there wasn't a locking mechanism in the door when she turned the key.

Lola stood and watched her aunt. She was about to ask if Phyllis was pulling her leg, but something in her aunt's facial expression made her keep quiet.

Phyllis closed her eyes, took a deep breath, and said, "Lola, I need you to close your eyes and sing a song for me. Any song, it doesn't matter. Will you do that?"

I'll humor her. "Sure, okay. How about Mary had a little lamb?"

"Perfect. Go ahead."

Lola closed her eyes and started singing. Meanwhile, Phyllis took another deep breath, closed her own eyes, and turned the key in the lock. She then told Lola to open her eyes. The door opened again, but this time it opened onto a green pasture on a sunny day. Off in the distance, they could see sheep. Lola stood there, dumbfounded. She looked at Phyllis to confirm what she was seeing and to ask if she could go through the door. Phyllis nodded, and they went through. She had no idea where she was, but she was no longer in the house, that was for sure.

"Where are we?" was all Lola could utter.

"We're in the Highlands of Scotland," Phyllis responded.

"Is this real?" A thousand questions were whirling through Lola's mind.

"Yes, it is."

Lola took in the sights as she rotated. When she couldn't see the door, she panicked.

"Phyllis, where's the door? How do we go back?" squeaked Lola.

Phyllis chuckled, put a hand on Lola's shoulder, and reassured her niece. "Don't worry. The door appears when you hold out a key, no matter where you are."

"But won't people see it and wonder what kind of crazy magic this is? That's what one part of my brain is asking right now," inquired Lola.

"Yes, it's best to arrive and leave discreetly. We try to find remote locations where there aren't a lot of people milling about. Like an alley, a deserted park, an empty parking lot. There are a few other rules and instructions, but this was the best way I had to explain the key to you. I'm sorry about scaring you," said Phyllis sympathetically.

"Holy shit! Sorry! I mean Leaping Lizards!" exclaimed Lola.

"It's okay. I think I had a similar reaction when I was shown."

Lola took a few steps. She kneeled and touched the grass. It seemed real enough. She moved to some wildflowers and inhaled deeply. It brought a smile to her face. She did another full 360 before she asked, "How old were you?"

"I was thirteen. That's the usual age for everyone in the family. Except you, because you weren't here then. Also, because of my epilepsy, I wasn't allowed to travel by myself. That's why it was so tense between Simon and me when we were kids. Our parents always expected him to accompany me on my adventures, and all he wanted to do was paint or visit art galleries."

They started walking down to a stream. In the distance, Lola could see fields with crops and farmers working in them. "Can they see us? Don't they wonder where we came from?" asked Lola. Phyllis only laughed at this.

"Can anyone use the key?" Lola said in wonder.

"No, only those from the Evers bloodline who have been given their own key can use it."

"Does the key only open doors to real places?" asked Lola. Then added quickly, "Can I go to Narnia? Does it only go to places in this time? Could I go back in time?"

She was about to voice a few more questions when Phyllis cut in with, "Those are all good questions! I've only ever been to real places in this time. We'll have to check the Archives."

"The Archives?" asked Lola. They had reached the stream, and Lola just had to put her feet in the water. She took off her shoes and socks, checked that the water looked okay, and waded in up to her knees. It felt glorious!

"The book that's passed down to Custodians. It explains everything, but it's in such old English that it's easier to explain it verbally than have you read it to discover your heritage!" was Phyllis' response.

Phyllis imitated Lola and waded into the stream as well. She almost lost her balance when Lola said, "If I could go back in time, I could get to know my father!"

Phyllis steadied herself, seemingly getting used to the uneven terrain. "Lola, I believe it might be possible. Your father was working on *something* in the months before he died. He never discussed it with me, but he poured over the Archives for hours and hours. He said the Archives had spells in them, so I thought he was looking for a cure or a way to extend his life somehow. A few years ago, I got the distinct impression that someone had been in his room. I asked Marie if she had moved anything, but she claimed all she did was dust, and I'm inclined to believe her. I asked Jackson if he'd been in Simon's room, and he said he hadn't. When I could come up with another explanation, I let it go and chalked it up to an overactive imagination," explained Phyllis, like she was still trying to work it out in her mind. They got out of the stream and sat in the grass, enjoying the sunshine.

Lola was itching to know the rest. "And then?" she prodded.

"Sometimes, when I miss him, I like to go look at his paintings. About six months ago, I sat in the armchair and noticed one of the paintings was sticking out in the stack under the window. I got up to investigate and, sure enough, it was a brand-new painting!" Phyllis paused for effect, and Lola gasped. "I couldn't discuss it with anyone outside the Evers family, and since I was alone, it was driving me crazy!" Phyllis grabbed both of Lola's hands and continued excitedly, "I think Simon found a way to travel ahead. I can't be sure. He might still be working out if it's safe to interact with people of a different time."

At this, Lola smiled and offered, "From what I've read in fiction books, two versions of the same person can't exist in the same time-space. Since dad's not alive in our time, it's probably safe for him to interact with us."

Phyllis was nodding. "That's assuming we don't keel over in a dead faint! Maybe he's been popping in and out of our timeline trying to figure out exactly when you would arrive here," she offered.

Lola was lying on her back, looking up at the sky, trying to get her mind around all this information. She looked over and saw that Phyllis was staring at the stream and wearing a goofy grin. Lola imagined it was probably at the thought of seeing her brother again or of witnessing the meeting between her and her father. All of a sudden, Lola sat up.

"If he can travel ahead in time, he might also be able to travel back in time. Maybe he used the key to look in on me while I was growing up, and I didn't even know it!" she said excitedly.

"And he might have been popping in to see me all this time too!" cried Phyllis.

Lola got up and started pacing and taking deep breaths to steady herself. *This is so exciting*! Ideas were racing through her mind. "We have to get a message to him. Maybe leave a note in his room with a date for him to focus on, and we'll meet him then," suggested Lola.

Phyllis put her socks and shoes back on and got up too. "I think we should do a little research first," she cautioned. "I'm sorry to bring this up, but what if it's not your father. What if it's a ghost or an intruder?" she said worriedly.

Lola waved this away as pure lunacy, but she stopped pacing as a thought dawned on her. "I can't tell Jackson about any of this, right?" She plopped back down on the grass and put her socks and shoes on.

"That's right. Though he feels like part of the family, he isn't. Well, not yet anyway." Phyllis extended a hand and hoisted Lola up from the ground, threaded her arm through Lola's, and they started walking again. It was such beautiful countryside, and the air was fresh and crisp.

They were quiet for a while before another thought occurred to Lola. "You said only those from the Evers bloodline have a key. Has a key ever been taken away?" she inquired as she got up.

"Yes. There are only a handful of keys. As you know, kids under thirteen don't have keys. And those who are deceased no longer have keys. There are usually no more than six keys in circulation. We have a total of ten keys, which is more than enough for three generations of adult Evers living at one time in the mansion. Custodians are keepers of the keys and the Archives. If the Custodian believes one of the Evers is not using his or her key appropriately, he or she may revoke the key," explained Phyllis.

Perplexed, Lola stared at her aunt and asked, "But what if the family member won't give it back?"

"They don't have a choice." Phyllis laughed. "You see, it's an incantation. The keys are magic, obviously. When the Custodian says the Revoking Incantation, the keys go back in the Repository. That's a fancy word for the box we keep the keys in," she added.

Lola was enthralled. Magic keys, incantations, repository? This was too incredible and wonderful at the same time. She felt like Harry Potter when he saw a wand in action for the first time.

"But what if the Custodian is the one who is not following the rules?" asked Lola.

"Then his key would automatically be revoked, and a new Custodian would be chosen."

Lola's curious mind needed to know everything. "How?" she asked.

"When Simon died, his key, the Repository, and the Archives appeared at the Attorney's office. For centuries, the Radcliffs have been responsible for transferring the keys and the book to the next Custodians. They cannot open the box or the book without an Evers present. They do know it's magic because it appears in their vault when a Custodian dies or if a Custodian must be revoked for whatever reason," said Phyllis.

"So, anyone who works in their office can see it pop up in their vault?"

"No, only an attorney from the Radcliff bloodline who's received special training," explained Phyllis.

Lola smiled to herself as she imagined Edward Radcliff wearing a

Jedi robe and scaling a wall while holding the Archives under his arm. "What's the special training?" asked Lola.

Phyllis was getting a crease between her eyebrows. She was clearly unprepared for so many questions. Nonetheless, she replied to Lola's question, "I don't know, but I assume it's something that's passed down in their family the same way the keys and the book are passed down in ours." Anticipating yet another question from Lola, she added, "I'm sorry I can't be more forthcoming. I was never meant to be Custodian, so I was never prepared adequately for the duties. And I admit I haven't been all that interested beyond the ability to travel the world. I've only been taking effective medication for the last twenty years or so. And I didn't travel much while your father was ill. Also, I was always worried about leaving once I was the only Evers left in the house. That's why I had Jackson install all those security features."

Another thought dawned on Lola. "Oh, that's why your room is so full of souvenirs! That means we can bring things back through the door?"

Phyllis stopped walking and turned to look at Lola with a serious look. Lola could feel bad news coming!

"No, you can't. You can only bring back what you had on you going in," said Phyllis sternly.

"Then how did you bring those things back?" asked Lola.

"I don't want to get into all the details just yet. Suffice it to say that I had them shipped here in the usual manner."

"But you can take pictures with your phone, right?" asked Lola.

"It's getting really tricky with social media and location services. People know where you are and what you're doing all the time. However, while everyone is taking pictures of their food at breakfast, I might be eating fresh croissants in Paris," added Phyllis with a wink.

"Right. Okay. I think I'm getting it. I can't wait to read the book," said Lola, deep in thought.

"That's another issue. You can't handle the book. Only I can, but you can stand next to me while I read it, I think. To be honest, I've never even opened the book," she said sheepishly. "When Edward came over with the keys and the book, I put them in the safe and forgot about them. They reminded me too much of Simon and how he left me here alone to deal with all of this." She looked down at her hands and added, "You must think I'm a total flake!"

Lola went over and gave her aunt a hug and said, "I can imagine how you felt. I'm freaking out just hearing about it. I'm sure you've done the best you could and, now that I'm here, you'll never be alone again."

At this, Phyllis smiled at Lola through teary eyes and wrapped her in another hug. "You are the best gift my brother could have ever given me."

Phyllis stepped back but held out her hand to Lola, and they resumed their stroll. "And now you know why it's best if you stay here for your schooling and don't have a job. You don't need the money, and you'll need a lot of time to research and study this."

Phyllis was wringing her hands a bit, probably hoping Lola would accept this news.

"Of course, I'll let Xavier know today that I won't be able to work after this week. I think he may suspect because he only agreed to a one-week trial."

"He knows your family is wealthy and that you wouldn't take a job from someone who needs it. But he also knows all teenagers need their independence and need to learn the value of an honest day's work. I believe both those goals have been achieved this week."

Lola thought for a moment. "Maybe I should donate my salary for the week. Any ideas as to where?"

"I think the library or school would be excellent choices. I was going to suggest it, but I'm proud you came up with it yourself." Phyllis was beaming, obviously happy that Lola was proving to be quite resilient.

"The library sounds good to me!" exclaimed Lola happily.

"Well, that's settled. Is there any place you'd like to visit before we go back home? To practice while I'm here with you?"

"Hmmm, let me see. I should choose somewhere that's not crowded, right? Where we won't show up out of nowhere," mused

Lola. Then she put some serious thought into it. *Where does one go when one has the power to go anywhere?*

"Yes. I find choosing a spot in nature helps, and I don't need a specific address."

"Okay. How about a secluded beach in Maui?" suggested Lola.

Phyllis took the key out of her pocket, and instantly the door appeared. Even though she'd been forewarned, Lola couldn't believe her eyes. She walked towards the door and put out her hand to touch it, and, thinking better of it, turned to check with her aunt. Phyllis nodded, and Lola touched the door. It was the same door, the one from the attic. She stepped to the side and peered behind the door; all she could see was the grass they'd just been walking on. *Incredible.*

Phyllis smiled as she watched Lola's obvious awe and glee. Eventually, she cleared her throat to get Lola's attention.

"Alright. Close your eyes, take a deep breath, and clear your mind. This is why practicing daily meditation and yoga helps. Now get a clear picture of where you want to go. Then put the key in the lock and turn it once counterclockwise until you hear a click. Then, remove the key and put it in your pocket."

Lola did as Phyllis instructed. When the door opened, there was the beach! She had no idea if it was a beach in Maui—it wasn't like there was a sign or anything. They walked through the door, and as Phyllis closed it, it disappeared. Lola had a slight moment of panic, but Phyllis took her hand and told her not to worry. They took off their shoes and socks and walked along the beach.

Then a very important question came to Lola. "How does time work on the other side of the door? While we are here, does time keep going back at home, or does it stand still like in Narnia?"

Phyllis laughed and explained, "Time is the same. The door is like a quick access portal. Which means the trips have to be short if you don't want to be missed. And if you don't plan them out, you might have money or identification on you. Our predecessors worked out a system for having money and lodging if they wanted to travel for longer periods. They purchased apartments or small homes in various cities all over the world. Over the years, we've equipped the homes with custom-made padlocks which open with the Evers key, and each of the homes is maintained by a weekly cleaning service. It's much easier than having to keep full-time staff when we are barely there. In a wall safe, we keep cash, emergency credit cards and cell phones, and copies of our passports. With the phone, you can always call home, if there is an Evers in residence, to get you out of a jam. Simon would do it all the time! It was easier to leave for extended periods if you didn't have a job or went to school."

They kept walking and talking about Phyllis' trips until it was time to go back for lunch and to get to Lola's job.

Phyllis turned to Lola and said, "To go home, simply take out the key and focus on the attic door and stairs in your mind. The door will appear."

Lola followed the instructions, and the door appeared. They opened the door, and voilà, they were back in the attic stairwell. Lola made a mental note to ask Phyllis about the apartments and houses she mentioned.

CHAPTER 22
APARTMENT

AFTER LUNCH, Lola headed for the garage to meet Jackson. He had her sit in the driver's seat, start the car, drive around the driveway, and practice turning, then back up. How thrilling and scary at the same time! They switched places, so he could drive to work and told her that they would practice actual driving the following week.

Jackson asked about her visit to the third floor. Lola said she got all worked up for nothing and that it was just a bunch of dusty antiques, furniture, and knick-knacks passed down through generations. It would be a history buff's dream come true, for sure. But Lola wasn't really into that sort of thing. She asked if Jackson had ever been up there, and he said no. As a child, he was told it wasn't safe. And since then, well, he didn't have a key to the third floor, so the point was moot.

LOLA ENJOYED her shift at the Food Lion. Today, Xavier had her stock shelves, bag groceries for clients, wash the street-facing windows, and gave her a rundown on how to operate the cash register. It was almost time to go, and Lola asked if she could talk to Xavier. As expected,

Xavier wasn't surprised that Lola would not be continuing and seemed quite pleased when Lola asked him to make her paycheck payable to the Possum Public Library. He even offered to bring it over himself and let them know she had donated it to them. Lola was embarrassed, but she agreed because she needed to get used to this kind of thing. And besides, this was her donation. She had earned the money, not her family, and she was quite proud of herself. They agreed she would come to work Thursday, as discussed.

Jackson was waiting for her on the sidewalk when she came out. He inquired as to how her shift had gone, and just as she was about to tell him about donating her paycheck, she heard someone call out her name. She turned and saw Bonnie skating towards them, waving her free arm while clutching a huge volume in her other one.

"Hey, guys! Are you going to the dance on Friday?"

Lola had no idea, so she looked at Jackson.

"Way to go, Bonnie. You completely killed my surprise. I was going to invite Lola to be my date," whined Jackson.

"Oh, sorry, Jack. That means yes, right? Lola? You in? We can go together if you want. You don't need a date."

Jackson looked crushed and began pushing a pebble with his shoe.

Lola laughed. She liked Bonnie. She was so spontaneous and energetic outside the library!

"How about this. I'll check my schedule with Phyllis and see if she's already made plans. Where can I reach you?" asked Lola.

Lola and Bonnie exchanged numbers and promised to get in touch later that night. Lola and Jackson watched Bonnie skate away, and soon, they too were on their way.

On the drive home, they discussed the dance. It was a formal event celebrating the official start of summer. Lola asked why it wasn't held on the Summer Solstice, and Jackson explained that's when they held prom, so it was a conflict of interest. Besides, it wasn't a Solstice celebration. It was the opening of the summer social calendar.

Lola decided she needed to keep a clear head about this suitable match thing. Jane and Phyllis would have advice about this. It's not that she didn't trust Jackson, but she could see why he'd have more than one reason for wanting her to commit to him early in the game. He may be nonchalant about it, but she could tell Jackson wanted to keep his job and stay where he was. Sure, she could also tell he liked her a lot. But that was a bonus. Wasn't it?

When they got back, Jackson asked if she wanted to see his apartment. Curiosity got the better of her, and she promptly agreed.

They went up the stairs, and Lola braced herself for messy boy syndrome. But the apartment looked clean to her, other than some dirty dishes in the sink, a towel on the floor in the bathroom, and some clothes piled on top of a chair in the bedroom. Oh, and an empty pizza box on the living room table. It could be worse. He picked up the offending articles along the way as they went from room to room, and soon the apartment was company-ready. It was nothing fancy, but the furniture was practical and the decor neutral. It looked lived-in, but you couldn't decipher anything about him by looking at it. She wished she could have seen his room in his parent's house. That would have told her a lot about him.

He asked if she wanted a soda, and they sat in the living room on the three-seater. They talked about their childhoods, best friends, their parents, and how they felt since their deaths. Everything but their potential *arranged* marriage.

All too soon, it was time for Lola to change and have dinner with Phyllis. She would have loved to continue their talk, but she also had a ton of questions for Phyllis and looked forward to resuming that conversation too.

Before she left, Jackson asked if she wanted to come back and hang out after dinner. Lola said she'd check with Phyllis and text him if she was free.

CHAPTER 23
TALK

AFTER DINNER, Lola had enough of Key and Archive talk and needed a break. She texted Jackson, and he said she should come right over. They sat on the sofa and listened to music, keeping the mood light. But when Jackson mentioned the dance and the possible matches she might meet, Lola didn't even see the point.

"It's been said, out loud, that I'm supposed to marry you. Not obligated, but strongly recommended. I mean, after what you said, it kind of follows that if we don't marry each other, one or both of us will die. I would only die AFTER I had a kid, of course. Otherwise, I couldn't *perpetuate* the Evers line," Lola said, rolling her eyes dramatically. Jackson got up to get them a couple of sodas.

"I'd like to say you're wrong or exaggerating, but I agree," he said gravely as he handed her a can and sat down again.

Lola felt like she was about to hyperventilate. She got up and started pacing and wringing her hands.

"But it's so messed up. How are we supposed to know if we have real feelings for each other? You might think I only want to be with you because you take care of the books, and I might think you want to be with me because of the money," she shrieked as she waved her hands about.

Jackson stood up too, and Lola could see he was trying not to laugh. This was, after all, very serious, and she had just been hit with all this information in less than two days. He took a breath, put his hands on her shoulders, and spoke slowly, "Lola, I don't need money. My parents left me a respectable sum of money. I have a great job here; I do get paid, you know. And if for some reason I lost this job, my college tuition is already paid for, and I could get ten others like it after I graduate, or I could do something else entirely, live anywhere in the world. Yes, I love it here, it's my home. But I'm not a prisoner to the job or a slave to the money. I chose this. And though it seems counterintuitive, you'll need to choose it too."

"What do you mean? I can't choose it. It's chosen for me!" wailed Lola.

He put his hands on either side of her face. "But you are mentally resisting it. Second-guessing yourself. The best thing you could do is accept your fate, embrace it if you can, and learn to see the positive aspects of the situation instead of the negative aspects," he said calmly.

Lola blinked. "What do you mean?" she said, calmer now.

He dropped his hands and stepped back as he explained. "Well, obviously, the fact that you now have a home and family is a positive aspect. The fact that you are now wealthy also doesn't hurt. But think about the time and energy you'll save not having to date and meet unsuitable matches in the hopes of finding true love. In many countries around the world, arranged marriages are still the norm," he said encouragingly.

Lola shook her head in denial. "But that's archaic at best," she said.

Jackson took on his lecturer tone, and started gesturing as he talked. "Not at all. Young people are now asking their parents to find them a list of suitable matches because dating today is much too hard and time-consuming. It takes time away from what matters, like your education or your job, or even the hobbies and passions you cultivate in your free time. Sure, you could meet someone on your own, at school, or in your extracurriculars. They might have similar interests and come from a similar background, both of which are important factors for a successful marriage. But if it doesn't work out, you have to deal with the emotional strife of a break-up at the most inopportune time, like during midterms or finals or before a big competition. Or, if it does work out and you fall in love, you might let your studies slip to spend more time together. Some people even quit school because they want to start a family. With an arranged marriage or a list of matches, you could use that time to get to know each other build trust and communication skills. You don't spend time worrying if that person has ulterior motives, if they are suitable, or after your money or connections. They've already been screened and pre-qualified. All that's left to decide is whether or not there is chemistry," he exclaimed.

"But what about love?" Lola protested. "I've never been in love, let alone dated anyone. I don't know what I want, but I know I want to decide for myself," she stated stubbornly.

"Ah, love!" Jackson sighed. "It's very important. But did you know that any two people can fall in love no matter who they are? I read an article in The New York Times a couple of years ago entitled *To Fall in Love With Anyone, Do This*. It was based on psychologist Arthur Aron's studies, which succeeded in making two strangers fall in love in his laboratory. The strangers sat for ninety minutes, face to face, and answered a series of increasingly personal questions. Then they had to stare silently into each other's eyes for four minutes. Interestingly enough, six months later, two participants were married. Hence, two compatible people could take the quiz and fall in love," said Jackson, pleased with himself.

Lola was dumbfounded. "That's amazing! It's incredible, yet it kind of explains how different people can fall in love and still be happy, or even how friends who are different stay friends for a lifetime."

"Exactly. As for us, I think we have chemistry, we've been pre-qualified, we already like each other, and if you didn't trust me, you wouldn't be here with me right now, alone in my apartment, after dark. If you're really worried about it, why don't you ask the attorney and your aunt to come up with a list of suitable matches in the community, some you're likely to meet at the dance this weekend. That way, you'll have choices, or at the very least, people to compare me to," Jackson said with a wink.

Lola was nodding. This seemed like a very good plan indeed. He was being much too cool about this. A testament to his maturity and sophistication. "Wow, thanks. That's a great idea. Aren't you worried I might like someone better?" Lola grinned slyly at him.

"I like my chances. I have a greater opportunity to woo you as we practically live together," he stated.

"But if it's practically arranged, isn't wooing irrelevant?" asked Lola.

Jackson looked at her in surprise. He feigned abhorrence by placing a hand over his heart and looking utterly shocked. "Wooing is NEVER irrelevant. It's one of the first things my parents taught me when I was old enough to understand it. And even before they started hammering me on gentlemanly conduct, just looking at them was enough to figure out they were doing it right. You could tell they were still as in love and attracted to each other as ever. My parents had an arranged marriage, and they were grateful for it every day of their lives," he said.

"Oh, that's why you're on board with this. I get it." Lola looked pensive then asked, "Wait, did my parents have an arranged marriage?"

Jackson shook his head. "No, I don't think so."

"So that means my dad was never supposed to marry my mom and have me. Doesn't that change everything? For you and me, I mean. I'm not the heir I was supposed to be if you get my meaning."

"I do! Like if your dad had married who they had planned for him to marry, he might have had two kids, and the eldest might have been a boy, and then I couldn't have married him," said Jackson, frowning.

"This is hurting my brain!" exclaimed Lola, holding her head.

"Never mind all that. Fate has still brought us together, now. And we've got two years to get to know each other before you have to take over as Custodian, and a few more until there is any talk of marriage and years yet before kids. Let's not jump the gun."

"You're right, of course. My imagination tends to get away from me, and I'm off into endless possibilities."

"You're a dreamer, that's good. The Custodian needs to have a vision and be somewhat of a risk-taker. But they should also be grounded and realistic," explained Jackson.

Lola rolled her eyes. "But those are complete opposites!"

"That's why the heir gets married! Because two heads are better than one. I'm super grounded, and though I have plenty of ideas, I tend to be a little too focused on the bottom line," stated Jackson.

"Which is also very important if you're meant to make the Estate prosper. I see your point. Our differences make us stronger as a team. But about those questions, maybe we should try to answer them."

"It's getting late, and there's no rush. I'm pretty sure we'll get to most of them on our own. But you can Google them if you're curious," suggested Jackson.

"I will!" Lola said as she nodded her head.

Jackson got up and said, "Come on, I'll walk you back to the house."

CHAPTER 24
ARCHIVES

LOLA SPENT the next morning in the study with Phyllis looking over the Archives. Written in a much older form of English, it wasn't light reading. They found a few pages that had been marked with a star in pencil, all about the concept of time. They surmised that Simon had been looking into it. If only he had left some notes. *A note, that's what we should leave.*

"Phyllis, we should write a note to my father and put it in the book and see if he responds!" exclaimed Lola.

"Why didn't I think of that? We could get some kind of binder set up, and you could write in it whenever we have a message or a question," suggested Phyllis while tapping a finger to her lips in reflection. "Also, we could do some research on the concept of time. That seems to be where Simon left off," she added.

Since Phyllis had some things to attend to, Lola volunteered to do research on her computer and, later, she could try the local library and even get Bonnie to help out, saying it was research for a paper she was trying to write for extra credit over the summer.

They went their separate ways and agreed to discuss the topic further at dinner.

After lunch, Jackson knocked on Lola's door and asked if she wanted to leave early, go into town, and get her learner's permit. She agreed, and they set off. They stopped to see Phyllis and have her sign the consent form. On the drive into town, they reviewed the manual so she could pass the written test. Lola had read it back home when Jane had gotten hers, so she was pretty up to speed. She aced the test, and Jackson said she was now ready to hit the road.

SHE WENT in for her last shift at the Food Lion. Today, in honor of her last day, and because he figured this might be of some use to her, Xavier showed her the books and had her practice inputting orders, receipts and expenses on the computer. Then he left her alone to man the store for about thirty minutes. She really didn't have to be worried as absolutely no one showed up in his absence.

All too soon, it was time to go. She gave Xavier a hug and thanked him for the opportunity. She also said she would be available if he was ever in a jam.

Jackson picked her up, and they went home, where Lola couldn't wait to show Phyllis her new learner's permit!

CHAPTER 25
SHOPPING

ON FRIDAY, Lola and Phyllis spent the day in Williamsburg. It was a quick tour because they had to shop for a dress for Lola and get their hair and nails done for the dance. Phyllis had already bought two suitable dresses for Lola, and both fitted perfectly, but she thought it might be fun for Lola to pick her own. After all, if they found something better, then great. Otherwise, they were all set. Williamsburg was a vibrant city, full of history, color, and charm. It was a far sight more interesting than Baltimore.

Phyllis took her to small shops in out-of-the-way corners of town. Most had one-of-a-kind gowns that could be fitted quickly on demand. Most of them knew Phyllis and were quick to serve tea, cakes, and even champagne when she arrived. They were all gushing about Lola and how pretty she was, and so she got the royal treatment. She found three gowns she liked and could not decide which she preferred. Phyllis had an easy solution—take them all, of course! That way, she'd have more options to accommodate her mood or comfort level on a given night. Besides, Phyllis added, she had many more events to attend and could not wear the same dress to those that were close together as there would be photographers in attendance. Madame Beaufort proudly told Lola that Phyllis always made it to the style pages. Phyllis laughed and said that it was mostly because her outfits were on the outlandish side, not necessarily because they were trendy.

"Madame Beaufort, please tell me these gowns are conservative and appropriate. I don't want to stand out. I just want to fit in," pleaded Lola.

"Aren't you precious, child!" she replied. "I would never let you leave here with an ill-fitting or inappropriate gown, Cherie. Your aunt has provided me with your social calendar, and I know all the important people in the area. I know exactly what you should or should not wear to any event! You can put your styling trust in me. Besides, I could tell right away when I saw you that you are not your aunt. Phyllis was always a headstrong girl. It was a bit of a chore dressing her when she came with her mama."

"Oh really? Phyllis always looks gorgeous and put-together to me!"

Madame Beaufort chuckled and said, "Cherie, the stories I could tell you! But I'll let Phyllis tell you herself. Better yet, you should look at the photo albums."

"Now, now. It wasn't that bad," Phyllis said, trying to defend herself. "I just knew at an early age that I was not meant to blend in. It was very difficult on my mama, who was very traditional and conservative."

"Ah yes, your mother was a pillar of the community and will be remembered fondly. She was known across three states for her hats alone. Lola, be sure to look at her collection!"

"I will, thanks," said Lola gratefully.

Madame Beaufort had the gowns pressed and packed while Lola and Phyllis went to get their hair and nails done. Then they had tea at the harbor front cafe and waited for Jackson to pick them up.

WHEN THEY GOT BACK, Lola spent some time relaxing in her room. She'd been on the go since she got here and hadn't had much downtime. Strangely she was nervous about the dance. Though it wasn't a ball, and she wouldn't have to do any fancy dances, she would be expected to join in on the fun with the other teenagers. There would be slow dancing and regular dancing, neither of which Lola had much experience with, especially all dressed up. To her, this felt like prom night. Everyone would have eyes on her—the new girl. And because she was the heir to the Evers Estate, she would draw even more attention to herself. Not to mention Phyllis would be discussing her with other important ladies in the hopes of drawing up a list of suitable event escorts and marital matches. Some of the mothers would already have their sons on alert, and she would have to make conversation with a bunch of strange boys all evening. Lola knew she babbled when she was nervous. But Phyllis had told her to be herself and that she had no one to impress. If anything, it was the mothers and their sons who needed to impress them. She would not have to spend time with people she didn't like or admire.

Later that evening, Phyllis and Lola had a simple dinner in the dining room. Phyllis ran her through the evening's schedule, the list of people they would likely be meeting, and a few names to look out for.

At 7:30 p.m., Jackson arrived looking sharp in a dark gray suit with a light blue-green shirt a few shades lighter than his eyes, open at the neck, and no tie. He looked gorgeous! After exclaiming that the ladies looked and smelled divine, he gave them each a peck on the cheek. It was time to go!

CHAPTER 26
DANCE

THE DANCE WAS HELD at the Possum Historical Museum. It was a lovely old mansion, though much larger than the Evers.' The ground floor held at least ten rooms, including the ballroom and a huge formal dining room.

Upon arriving, guests were offered a guided tour, and Lola went with Jackson while Phyllis went to catch up with old friends. Now was not the time for introductions, and this would be a great way to familiarize herself with her surroundings and scope out the competition. Not that she was competing with anyone, she just wanted to see what the other kids her age were wearing and how they were acting. They were used to this type of social gathering. She was not.

Jackson kept a firm grip on her arm; he could tell she was nervous and needed the extra reassurance. Since the guide was keeping up a constant monologue, they didn't need to interact with anyone else in the group. She relaxed a little and started paying attention to what he was saying about the museum and about the town's history.

When the tour was over, they went to join Phyllis. Lola was by now feeling much better. From her observations, she knew she was well dressed, certainly among the best, but not in a way that drew too much attention to her. People were giving her furtive glances, not outright stares. That was good. She tried to keep a smile plastered on her face.

Phyllis asked if she was ready, she nodded, and they were off. They made the rounds, as it was called, while the first wave of dances hit the floor. These were ballroom dances, so Lola wouldn't miss a thing. She met some interesting people, a few good-looking and courteous boys, a few bores, and one or two pompous asses. She was expecting more of those. The mothers were okay, too. After about thirty minutes, they took a break and retreated to the refreshments table. Lola spotted Bonnie and excused herself from her aunt to go see her.

"Bonnie! Hi, it's good to see a familiar face!" she greeted her.

"Lola!" Bonnie exclaimed, giving her a hug. "When did you get here?"

"I got here at eight, but I did the guided tour, and then I made the rounds with my aunt. I've escaped for now, but there should be another round soon!"

"You're funny! At the risk of freaking, you out, how about a round of introductions, Bonnie-style?" suggested Bonnie.

"Why not? I'm all dressed up and don't know how to ballroom dance, so I might as well use my wits and charm!"

Bonnie took Lola first to meet her mom and sister. Her mom said she knew Phyllis well since they were on a committee together. Then Bonnie took her to meet some of her friends who were not hanging out with their parents. Jackson was in one of the groups and made some introductions of his own. As both Bonnie and Jackson were older than Lola, their friends were older as well, though some of them introduced their brothers and sisters who were Lola's age. There was no way she was going to remember all these names.

She was starting to get a little overwhelmed when a really good song started to play on the dance floor. Her face lit up, and she automatically looked for Jane, only to realize she wasn't there. Bonnie took notice and grabbed her by the arm, and yelled, "Come on, let's dance!" A bunch of people rushed to the dance floor and joined them. They kept playing songs Lola knew and liked, so they all stayed on the dance floor for at least an hour. Eventually, the DJ started playing oldies, and the kids were replaced by their parents.

Lola went to get something to eat and drink at the refreshment table with Bonnie and her friends, then to sit and relax until the next batch of songs played. After a while, Phyllis came to fetch Lola for another round of introductions. By then, Lola was ready for it as the conversation with Bonnie's friends revolved around people she didn't know, and she was feeling awkward again.

More parents and offspring were introduced to Lola. Some she had already met and could now match them to their parents. Everyone was warm and welcoming, and Lola started to relax again.

When the second round was done, it was already eleven o'clock. Soon, the DJ started playing Lola's kind of music again, and she went to find her new friends to dance. They danced for another hour before the DJ started playing slower, older songs again. Another round of refreshments and relaxing followed, but this one was short-lived. The band was playing slow songs, and one of the boys she had met came to ask her to dance. She didn't feel like she could refuse, so she agreed.

Unfortunately, this started a trend, and there were ten more after that! Then Jackson came to ask her to dance and said they'd be going soon because Phyllis was tired. He offered that if she wanted to stay, he could come back and get her later. Lola said she would leave at the same time as Phyllis, as it was almost one o'clock by then, and she was exhausted.

The song that was playing for her dance with Jackson was a more recent one that she liked, and she couldn't help humming along. After almost a dozen slow dances, she had just been going through the motions. But there was something in the way Jackson was holding her that sharpened her awareness. All of a sudden, her senses were on high alert, and as she looked up, she saw he was staring at her intently. A blush crept up her neck and invaded her face. She looked down again. He held her closer and put his face next to her ear. He smelled her hair and rested his cheek against it. It was such an intimate gesture, yet it felt almost natural. Lola relaxed and set her head on his shoulder, breathing in his scent. He smelled so good. His arms tightened around her, and one of his thumbs stroked her back to the beat of the song. She could have stayed in his arms forever. It felt warm, safe, right.

When the song ended, Lola sighed, smiled up at him, and thanked him for the dance. He took her hand and guided her to where Phyllis was chatting with some of her own friends. She must have been looking at them because she had one of her patient, happy smiles.

"Ready to go?" she said.

"Yes, I'm exhausted!" replied Lola. "I don't remember ever dancing or talking quite as much as I did tonight!"

"Did you enjoy yourself?" asked Phyllis as she looped her arm through Lola's, and they walked to the main entrance.

"Yes, I did. I can't imagine I'll remember anyone's name, but everyone was friendly." Lola put her hand over her mouth as she yawned and rested her head on Phyllis' shoulder as they waited for Jackson to bring the car around.

"I'm glad. Then this outing was a success! And you were a hit! Be prepared for a deluge of invitations in the coming weeks," said Phyllis in a single breath excitedly.

"Invitations? More dances?" squeaked Lola, slightly panicked.

"No, silly. Dinner parties, birthday parties, backyard BBQs, trips to the beach, that sort of thing," reassured Phyllis.

"Oh, that's not so bad," said Lola, relieved. Just then, Jackson pulled at the curb, and he came to open the door for them.

"It's summer, after all. You should have time to learn how to dance before your first actual ball. Don't fret." They got into the car and sped away into the night.

Lola put her head on the headrest and closed her eyes to think about her dance with Jackson. She was remembering how it felt to be in his arms, to be so close to him she could smell not only his after-shave but the faint smell of his soap and deodorant. Maybe it was because she grew up without a dad, but she loved those smells. They were somehow soothing. It's funny how smells could evoke strength and safety. Maybe she was just crazy. All she knew was that she was floating on a happy cloud, and she never wanted to come down.

SHE HAD such a feeling of weightlessness. It was uncanny. Like she was flying. This was one of those great dreams! She tried to turn onto her side and hit something firm, something that was not her pillow. She opened her eyes a crack to investigate and saw only darkness. However, she was moving! Was she awake or sleeping? She opened her eyes completely and saw that she was not in her bed; she was being carried. By Jackson, no less!

"What are you doing?" she squealed, wide awake and struggling in his arms.

"You fell asleep in the car. We tried to wake you, but you were dead to the world. Phyllis asked that I carry you up to your room," replied Jackson.

"Where are we now?" asked Lola looking around.

"We're in your room. I must have jostled you awake when I opened the door. Here, let me set you on the bed."

Lola grimaced and was glad Jackson couldn't see the blush heating up her ears. "What am I, six years old? I'm so embarrassed. You should have set me on the couch downstairs."

"Phyllis thought you would be more comfortable in your bed and wouldn't be alarmed if you woke in the night," added Jackson patiently.

"Right. Um, thanks." Lola was completely mortified. At least he hadn't tried to put her pajamas on!

"It was my pleasure. Truly. At least now you can get out of your gown and into your nightclothes," said Jackson with a grin.

"Yes, that'll be much more comfortable."

"Alright then, good night," said Jackson walking away.

"Wait. What would you have done if I hadn't woken up?"

"I would have removed your shoes, draped you with a throw blanket, and kissed your forehead." Jackson followed this with a giant wink.

"Sorry I missed that," said Lola, pouting.

"If you like, I can step outside while you change and get into bed, and then I can tuck you in," he suggested.

"Yes, please!"

She ran to her closet and changed into her nightclothes. Then she quickly washed her face, brushed her teeth, and combed out her hair. She ran back, hopped into bed, brought the covers up to her chin, and called out that she was ready.

He came back in with a chuckle. "That was fast! Well, well, well. Look at you!"

"What?" she asked, surprised.

"You look all of six years old in your pink pajamas."

"They're lilac, actually," she muttered.

"I figured you for the type who wore a beat-up t-shirt to bed."

"I was. But Phyllis bought all these nice clothes for me. When I tried these pajamas on, they were the softest, most comfortable thing I'd ever worn. I never wanted to take them off."

He sat down on the bed, tucked the covers on either side of her, and kissed her forehead. He lingered there for an instant like he was debating kissing her lips while he was there, but he must have decided against it.

"Good night, Lola," he said eventually.

"Good night, Jackson. Thanks for everything."

"You're welcome. Sweet dreams."

Lola closed her eyes with a smile and was asleep within minutes.

CHAPTER 27
SATURDAY

SHE WOKE with a start because someone was shaking her.

"What?!!?" she mumbled.

"Get up, lazybones, or you'll miss Pancake Saturday!" said Jackson.

"Go away. I just went to bed," said Lola, pushing his arms away and pulling the covers over her head.

"It's 10 a.m., an hour later than usual to compensate for our late arrival. Phyllis always makes pancakes on Saturdays. Get up, or you'll miss out!" he advised.

"Why are you in my room? Why are you so cheerful? Coffee, man. I need coffee!" implored Lola.

"Okay, so you're grumpy in the morning. Duly noted! There's coffee downstairs. The faster you get up, the faster you get coffee," he promised.

"All right, all right," mumbled Lola getting up. "Can I at least use the bathroom?"

"You have a minute; otherwise, I start tickling you," threatened Jackson.

That got a giggle out of her as she ran to the bathroom. She used the toilet, splashed some water on her face, brushed her teeth, and checked her hair in the mirror. *Good*, she thought, *at least I don't look terrible*. Then she wondered how long he had stood there, watching her sleep. She couldn't decide if this was cute or creepy.

When she came out of the bathroom, he was waiting in the sitting room. She grabbed her robe from the foot of the bed and joined him. They went down together, and Lola made a beeline for the coffee pot. Cup in hand, she headed for the kitchen, where she found Phyllis flipping pancakes like a pro. She gave them each a platter to set under the heating lamps. Lola had raspberry pancakes, and Jackson had plain ones. They came back for the next batch, which was chocolate chip, and one laden with scrambled eggs and bacon. On the sideboard, there were also fresh berries, hot chocolate sauce, real maple syrup, and whipped cream. This would be so good!

"Phyllis makes the best pancakes in the world," said Jackson in a reverent tone.

"Flattery will get you everywhere, young man!" replied Phyllis, amused.

"Oh wow, these *are* good!" said Lola with her mouth full of raspberry pancakes topped with everything she had found on the sideboard.

"I'm glad you like them. I gather you enjoyed yourselves last night?" asked Phyllis as she sat down to join them.

"It was a lot of fun. I met way too many people, but it felt good to dance. The music was pretty decent," answered Lola.

"Yeah, the DJ is a friend of mine. We went to high school together. He's studying dentistry at Raleigh, and he DJs in what little spare time he has," added Jackson.

"Is that Peter Marks? I know his parents. They have a lovely home in Virginia Beach," commented Phyllis.

"Yes, that's him," replied Jackson.

They chatted about the dance and the people Lola had met. Lola and Jackson offered to clear the table and clean up the kitchen, which Phyllis graciously accepted. She said she was going to tend to her garden and then thought she'd catch a nap in the gazebo. She suggested that Lola make use of the pool if she wanted. Lola thought that was a great idea since she could certainly get some laps in and work on her non-existent tan. She would probably go for a nap as well. Jackson said he might join her later in the pool if that was alright. He explained that he had a few chores to do first and then suggested they try an actual driving lesson later in the afternoon. Lola nervously agreed to this.

She went back to her room and looked longingly at her bed. Though cozier, the bed was no match for fresh air and sunshine. She put her swimsuit on, a tame one-piece, grabbed her goggles, sunglasses, and her book, threw on a cover-up and headed back downstairs. She stopped in the kitchen to grab a bottle of water and an apple in case she got hungry later and was too lazy to come back for food. Then she headed out. As she walked towards the back of the Estate, she spotted Phyllis in the vegetable garden.

"What's ripe?" she asked.

"Green beans, Swiss chard, a few plum tomatoes, and radicchio lettuce," replied Phyllis.

"Yum!" said Lola.

Phyllis saw Lola was heading for the pool. "I don't think we'll need lunch today. There's a fridge with beverages in the pool house and some snacks if you get hungry, but you're welcome to raid the kitchen if you want more sustenance. I'll be going on a short trip this afternoon if you take my meaning, But I'll be back in time for dinner. I've put a roast in the crockpot. I'll just add these vegetables before I go, and we'll be all set. Enjoy your afternoon!"

"Thanks, you too! I can't wait to hear about it."

"And I can't wait to hear about the boys from last night!" said Phyllis with a wink.

Lola chuckled at that and started towards the pool.

CHAPTER 28
POOL

JACKSON MUST HAVE DROPPED by because the umbrellas were open, and a couple of towels had been set on a chair. There was also a large-brimmed sun hat, some sunscreen, and a note:

Please apply sunscreen and wear a hat. Your pastiness is an invitation to sunburn. You'll thank me later. J.

It was cute that he cared. Between him and Phyllis, she really felt like she mattered. Like her well-being was of utmost importance. It felt good to be part of a family, such as it was. They were definitely a motley crew, though! The orphaned heiress, the epileptic guardian, and the caretaker betrothed.

She spread one of the towels on the chair and put her things on the table next to it. She debated going directly in the pool or getting some sun first. Remembering the note, she slathered some sunscreen all over herself, put on her shades and her new sunhat, and reclined on the chair to let the lotion sink in. Not surprisingly, she promptly fell asleep.

Somewhere deep in her subconscious, she felt something tickling her foot. She rubbed her other foot over it, but it kept coming back. Eventually, it woke her.

"Time to flip over."

"What!" said Lola groggily.

"You've been on your back for too long. You'll burn. Did you fall asleep again?" moaned Jackson.

"I guess I did. Do I already have a burn? I don't know how long I've been asleep."

"I was trimming hedges nearby and saw you lie down. It's been about twenty minutes. You should turn over," advised Jackson.

"I think I'll hit the pool," said Lola jumping to her feet.

"No problem. I'll go back to those hedges now and see you for a dip later."

"Okay, thanks for saving my skin," said Lola gratefully. "Literally!"

"No problem," said Jackson with a grin.

He left, and she dived into the pool. The water was surprisingly warm, and it was a good-sized pool. Before starting in on her laps, she rested her arms on the side of the pool and watched Jackson trimming the hedges. He'd taken off his shirt, and Lola was enjoying the view. He must have had earbuds in because his head was bobbing, and he seemed to be swaying a bit as he worked like he was dancing a bit. Jackson was really fit, Lola determined. He was lean but not thin. Toned, but not ripped. He turned to get a drink of water and saw Lola watching him. He smiled, raised a hand, and waved. Mortified, Lola gave a quick wave back and sank under the water. She swam for about twenty minutes, drank some water, and plopped down on her stomach for phase two of her nap. She hadn't even been there for two minutes when she saw a shadow cast over her.

"Let me put some sunscreen on your back, so you don't burn," a voice boomed over her.

"Are you being paid to watch over me like that? I half expect you to be standing there with a tissue if I sneezed!" said Lola somewhat sarcastically. She was still a little miffed that he'd caught her staring. Jackson was confident enough without the added knowledge that she was checking him out.

"No, I'm just a very interested party in your welfare," replied Jackson smiling innocently.

"Sounds serious," said Lola with a smirk. She grabbed the lotion and gave it to him, then turned her face into the chair so he could also reach the back of her neck.

"It is," said Jackson seriously. "I care about you, Lola."

Lola felt her pulse rate going up, but she didn't dare turn and look at him. "Oh, I, um, care about you too," she stammered. She was searching for something to add, but Jackson just kept talking, nonplussed.

"Besides, I'm older than you; I should be looking out for you. Kind of like an older brother" added Jackson proudly.

"If I had an older brother, I don't think he'd be putting suntan lotion on my back. At least, if he did, he wouldn't do it quite so......" Lola trailed off as Jackson's last comment seemed to catch up with him, and his strokes on her back became deeper, slower.

"Thoroughly?" quipped Jackson, hands suspended in the air.

"Never mind," mumbled Lola, thinking she probably imagined he was doing anything else than dutifully applying lotion as he would on any relative's back.

"No, what were you going to say?" prodded Jackson, resuming his application, but this time on the back of her arms.

"Sensually," she admitted, thankful that he couldn't see the flush on her face.

"Oh." Jackson's response was abrupt.

"Yeeeeaah." Lola drew her response out a lot more.

"I thought I was doing it in a detached, professional manner. But your skin is so soft and warm from the sun. I guess my hands got carried away. Sorry, should I stop?"

"No!" said Lola quickly. "It feels good. Really good," she admitted.

"To me too. Should I do your legs then?"

"Sure. I mean, if you want to," added Lola, trying to be nonchalant when she was feeling anything but. She really had no experience with this kind of thing.

"Trust me, I do." Jackson's voice had dropped an octave, and Lola's heart skipped a beat.

He drizzled lotion down the back of her legs as if it were hot chocolate sauce, and he planned on licking it off like in the movies. Then, one at a time, he massaged the lotion into each leg, running his hands slowly up her inner thigh and stopping just shy of touching her bathing suit. She gave an involuntary moan almost at the same time that one left Jackson's lips. *I wonder if he is feeling the heat between us too?* She turned her head to the side, and she noticed Jackson adjusting his pants and stuffed her face back in the towel. As if that was a silent signal, and before things got out of hand, he quickly moved down her legs and, since he had some lotion leftover, gave her feet a little massage.

"If this job doesn't pan out, you could always become a masseuse," said Lola trying to put her thoughts elsewhere.

"That good?" he smirked.

"Oh, yeah. Really good," moaned Lola.

"Not too......sensual?" quipped Jackson, trailing a finger down her foot with enough pressure, so it wasn't a tickle.

"Now that you mention it, I'm pretty sure that falls under the category of inappropriate and unprofessional." Lola giggled as she raised her head and looked at him.

"Oh, I'm sorry, Lola. Did I go too far?" Jackson asked, putting his hands up in surrender, looking guilty.

"I'm not complaining. I liked it. But if that was your job, then you'd be fired, obviously," said Lola in what she hoped was a flirty voice.

"But technically, I am on duty, and I've made inappropriate advances to my employer's niece. I could get fired," Jackson said worriedly.

"Inappropriate, perhaps, but they were neither unsolicited nor unappreciated," said Lola, her face now crimson.

"You're still very young and obviously inexperienced, Lola. I want to take my time with you," said Jackson in a soft, patient voice.

"And I appreciate both your restraint and your gentle manner. But you should know, I am attracted to you, and I felt things when we kissed, when we danced, and just now when you were applying lotion. I'm not a baby; I'll be sixteen next weekend. Most girls my age have already had sex, or at the very least been to all the other bases. I may be a virgin, but I have hormones like everybody else," stated Lola.

"And I'm nineteen, so technically going too far with you could lead to prosecution in certain states." Jackson stood up and crossed his arms.

"Yeah, well, consenting adults and all that," replied Lola.

"That's the point, Lola, you're not an adult therefore you cannot give informed consent."

"This conversation is killing my buzz," moaned Lola.

"That was the point," replied Jackson with a nod. "I needed a reality check. That's my cue. I'll go and do some more strenuous manual labor. I'll be back in an hour. Put some sunscreen on your front and turn over. You've been lying on your stomach for twenty minutes already."

"Yes, sir! But wait, don't you want to put the lotion on me? You're so good at it," said Lola impishly.

"Walking away, now," he said, backing off. "On second thought, I think I might jump in the pool to cool off before I head back." He strode purposefully toward the pool house and quickly returned in a bathing suit. Lola could only stare at him. She was starting to get up and join him when he pointed the finger at her. "Don't you dare get up off that chair until I'm back on the lawn," he said, trying to keep a straight face. He did a few laps, then got out of the pool and headed back to the pool house to change with a quick, "See you later!"

CHAPTER 29
DAYDREAMING

AFTER JACKSON LEFT, Lola went back into the water, just to cool off. Then she dutifully slathered on more sunscreen because she was sure he was lurking around somewhere. It was a little hot, so she went to sit under the umbrella to read her book. It was hard to focus at first. All she could think of was Jackson's hands on her thighs, gliding up and down, slowing between her legs and rounding near her bum. She was getting all hot and bothered again.

None of the other boys she met at the dance made her tingle all over as Jackson did. Of course, none of the other boys had kissed her. Sure, she had danced with a few of them; some had even kissed her cheek or hand. But it wasn't the same. She was sure there was something special about Jackson that had nothing to do with teenage hormones or first times. It felt destined. And that bothered her a bit. If the key was magic, then it could also be possible that they were all under some kind of spell that ensured the master plan unfolded in a certain way with the right actors in place. Both her parents and Jackson's ancestors seemed to have paid a high price for not following the plan. So far, the plan seemed pretty acceptable to Lola, but just because the cage was pretty didn't mean she was willing to live in it for the rest of her life. That was why she was taking her time in believing the whole traveling thing.

It seemed much too good to be true. Even wealth was a bit much for her. At least the developments with Jackson felt like something that happened to a normal teenager. Girl meets boy. Boy kisses girl. The girl goes all mushy. Normal. But an orphaned 15-year-old girl who suddenly becomes an heiress to a massive Estate AND a secret magic legacy all seemed way too over the top to Lola. She wasn't skeptical by nature and being an avid reader, she was not completely surprised by the plot twist in this story, but wasn't she past fairy tales and happy endings? There was a catch in here somewhere, and she was determined to find it before it found her. Meanwhile, she was just going to enjoy her new life, her new crush, and her new aunt. Just because she stayed real didn't mean she didn't appreciate all the blessings life had sent her way. Reading a book under the shade of an umbrella on a Saturday afternoon was way up there on the top ten things to be grateful for.

"Lemonade?"

Lola shrieked, and the book that was resting on her lap flew out of her hands. As she put her hands over her heart, she said breathily, "Stop sneaking up on me like that!"

"I didn't sneak up on you," said Jackson dryly. "You are way too deep in your own head. I called out your name from the pool house already."

"Oh, sorry. I guess I was deep in thought." Lola shrugged.

"Well, I brought you some lemonade. It's tastier than plain old water, and it will boost your electrolytes."

"Maybe you should study medicine. You're very concerned about my health," said Lola sarcastically.

"I did consider it at one stage but thought it could be a nice hobby instead. I like to read up on nutrition and exercise."

"Yes, I can see you are an exercise buff," said Lola appreciatively. "If I keep eating the way we do here, I'm going to have to think seriously about daily exercise. And not just yoga with Phyllis."

"What are you talking about? You're barely skin and bones,"

exclaimed Jackson as he gave her a once over. "You could use a few extra pounds."

"You don't seem to have any extra pounds," complained Lola. "You look like you train every day for hours."

"Thanks, I think. I can't tell if that's a compliment or not because your face is looking a little disdainful right about now."

"I think that's a cross between disgust and jealousy. No one should look like that outside of magazines. It makes the rest of us look bad!" said Lola with a pout.

"You're funny! I go for a run every morning and work out in the gym a few times per week. I also do laps in the pool every other night. It's not as hot then, and it relaxes me. You really can't beat the perks of this job. My duties sort of blend into my daily life, and I don't feel like I'm working at all. It just feels like a normal day to me. I think my parents felt that way too. Like we were all one big family."

"Except some of us live in the big house......Oh God, I can't believe I said that!" she added, her hands flying to her mouth. "I'm so sorry, Jackson."

"No, don't worry about it. It's just because you are not used to how things are yet. You didn't grow up here, in the house. You probably feel very uncomfortable having people do things for you and them be paid to do it," said Jackson matter-of-factly.

"You're right. Thank God there aren't any full-time servants, or perhaps I should say, employees."

Jackson was quiet for a moment, then said, "Phyllis feels that way too. It was okay when it was my parents because they felt like family. But now, it feels off to have Marie cleaning up after her. Marie is friendly and good at her job, but she's always felt temporary. She doesn't belong here like I do. I know that sounds weird."

"No, it doesn't. It sounds right. You do belong here. More than I do!" Lola pursed her lips at this admission.

"You'll grow into it," said Jackson confidently. Then he clapped his hands and added, "Alright, I am off the clock. Time for some R&R!" He got up and headed towards the pool. "Fancy a dip in the pool with me?"

"No dunking!" warned Lola.

"On my honor!" said Jackson, giving her a scout salute.

They spent the rest of the afternoon swimming and suntanning, reading, and even played a game of backgammon. By three, Lola had had enough of the sun and asked if they could have that driving lesson. Jackson agreed, and they decided to meet back at the garage about thirty minutes later after they had changed.

CHAPTER 30
MAXWELLS

THERE WAS a knock on her door. Lola checked her watch and wondered if she was running late. It was Jackson, there to give her a heads up that they had company.

"Oh? Who's here?" she said, intrigued, as she let him into the sitting room and put in her last earring.

"The Maxwells. Norma and Phil, and their two kids, Matthew, and Sheila."

Lola looked thoughtful. "The names seem familiar, but I can't place them." Lola was worried. She went back into her room to add a touch of mascara and gloss to her look. Jackson waited in the sitting room and pitched his voice so she could hear him.

"Sheila is my age, and Matthew is closer to yours. You met them at the dance. They're nice. I think you even danced with Matthew. He's very tall, has light blond hair that was slicked back like a German soldier, though he doesn't usually wear it like that." Lola giggled from across the room as she gave herself a last once over and joined Jackson in the sitting room.

"Yes! I remember him. He was a little stiff and formal. I kept thinking he was about to call me fraulein!" said Lola ruefully.

"He's just shy," Jackson said with a smile, "and I think his parents made a big deal about him trying to impress you."

"Poor guy! I hope he's more relaxed tonight!" said Lola, hoping the same for herself. She was getting used to dinner with Phyllis and sometimes Jackson. But guests would require more attention to table manners and conversation.

"Are you ready?" asked Jackson. Lola nodded, and he opened the door for her, and they went out into the hall.

"You can expect to have company for dinner more often from now on. The summer season has officially begun!" Jackson seemed genuinely excited about this. He had a big goofy grin on his face. They had paused near the staircase to finish up their conversation, and Lola admitted that his mood was contagious. *This might be fun!*

"Thanks for the heads up. I guess we should go down now. Do I look okay?"

"You look ravishing, as always!" The gleam in Jackson's eyes made her heart skip a beat.

"Flatterer!" she said, blushing, as she pretended to swat him.

"I was raised well. Come along, or they'll wonder what we're up to!" Jackson offered his arm, and they descended the stairs. As they neared the dining room, they broke apart naturally, and Jackson motioned that she should enter first as she was the guest of honor.

Dinner was a livelier affair with the extra guests. Indeed, both Matthew and Sheila were relaxed; it was Lola that was nervous since she didn't have near enough dinner conversation experience. She would need to brush up on local and world events to keep up with these people. It was an art form she had yet to master.

After dinner, the adults went into the parlor, and the teenagers went to the front porch. Seeing her pained expression, Jackson suggested a game of cards they all knew, and things were easier from there.

About an hour later, Norma and Phil came in to collect their offspring, and Matthew asked if she wanted to go see a movie with him later in the week. Lola wanted to decline but didn't know how to do it graciously. Jackson came to the rescue by reminding her that Jane was coming in on Thursday for the long weekend, so Lola invited them both to the 4th of July party they were hosting. Sheila said they would be delighted but had to check their social calendar to ensure their parents hadn't already accepted another invitation on their behalf. Now that was a gracious response! I should take notes, thought Lola. Or maybe I need a private tutor in diplomacy. The Maxwells left, and Phyllis headed to the study. Jackson asked Lola if she wanted to go for a short walk before going to bed, and they headed for the path.

It was a beautiful starry night. Jackson took her hand, and they walked in silence. In no time at all, they had looped back to the house, and Lola was amazed at how time flew when they were together. And this time, they hadn't even talked. Only held hands in the moonlight. It was so romantic! She liked that they could spend time together so easily. She never felt awkward with Jackson. Well, except when she saw him in his bathing suit. She just wanted to crawl under her towel and not come out. Jackson was definitely at ease in his skin. He didn't ever look unsure of himself. Maybe it was because he was older. Lola hoped she would grow into herself sooner rather than later. She certainly had a good role model in Phyllis.

They walked in through the mudroom door again, and Jackson kissed her goodnight. As Jackson pulled away, Lola found herself wishing they could kiss for longer, but Jackson, as if reading her mind again, said they needed a chaperone. He reasoned that they were spending way too much time alone together, and it was all he could do to keep himself in check. That pleased Lola because she was starting to think she was the only one feeling less than satisfied with their chaste kisses and fleeting touches. Jackson was a gentleman. She would give him that! He kissed her forehead and was off, leaving her feeling a little bereft.

CHAPTER 31
TRAVELING

LOLA STOPPED at the study to see if her aunt was still there, as she wanted to ask her some more about the key. Phyllis was indeed there and seemed pleased to see Lola.

"Phyllis, do you think Jackson and I are spending too much unsupervised time together?" ventured Lola, biting her lower lip, unsure of herself.

"No, of course not. Jackson is a good boy," Phyllis said with a patient smile. "I trust his behavior with you is appropriate. Isn't it?" added Phyllis as a worry line appeared between her eyebrows.

"Yes, it is. A little too much if you ask me!" said Lola despondently as she plopped down in the armchair next to her aunt.

Phyllis set down her book and shook her head. "Don't be in too much of a hurry to grow up. Enjoy these moments of romance and innocence. They end all too quickly, and you may well spend the rest of your life looking for glimpses of them." She took a sip from her drink and pointed at it to ask Lola if she wanted some. Lola declined; brandy or whiskey or whatever strong liquor was in her glass was not her thing.

"How very philosophical. Why didn't you ever marry?" she asked, genuinely curious. "If you don't mind me asking," she added quickly.

Phyllis waved her off before responding. "I had too many beaus to choose from! But none of them made my heart flutter," she said, then stared intently into the fire and added, "There was a man I liked, but it wasn't in the cards. I'll tell you about him some other time." Phyllis sighed and took another sip of her drink.

Lola decided to change the subject. "Okay. I had a question about the key."

"Yes?" inquired Phyllis expectantly.

"You were traveling today, right?" asked Lola.

"Yes, I was. I went to London to have tea with an old friend." Phyllis smiled, remembering tea at the Ritz. "It's so much fun talking about the key with you. It feels good to have someone to confide in after years of carrying the secret."

"I was wondering if I could use my key on the attic door at the same time as you?" said Lola hopefully.

"Oh, that's right. We didn't cover that!" Phyllis got up and walked around the room. "The simple answer is—yes. Technically, we don't even need the attic door at all. We could come and go from anywhere. However, since there are other people in the house and we can't be absolutely sure we'll be alone, you should use the attic door for a while," explained Phyllis. "Soon, you'll notice I often go up to my room for a nap. That way, Marie or Jackson know not to disturb me, and I know it's safe to come and go from my room." She stopped and leaned on the desk as she continued. "When you come back, if someone was using the door at that exact moment, there would just be a short delay until the door is closed again and can be used to come back home. I've never had an issue. When I was young, there were four of us using it, and there were never any problems," she finished.

"Oh, okay," said Lola relieved. "And how do you manage to keep it from other people?" she asked.

Phyllis pushed off the desk and came back to sit in the armchair next to Lola. "Well, I've lived alone for a long time. Marie and Jackson don't live here, and since they are technically my employees, I don't have to tell them anything. The house is big enough that if someone is looking for you, they might think you are in another part of the house or even on the grounds. But if I have houseguests, I'll just say I'm going to rest or read, and people don't usually disturb me."

"Sounds like a good plan. Should I let you know when I go?" asked Lola.

"For the first few times, I think you should. Just to be on the safe side," said Phyllis emphatically.

"Also, if someone found out on their own about the key, without us telling them, what would happen?" asked Lola nervously.

"Good question! I think Jackson's parents knew about the keys. They never said anything to me about it, and I don't think they told Jackson about it. We'll have to look that up in the Archives. We'll set some time aside for studying the book this week," said Phyllis.

"I'd like that. I would prefer to know more about all this before I start trekking all over the place," added Lola worriedly.

Phyllis looked fondly at her. "A very wise decision! You're putting a lot of thought into this. I admit I wasn't nearly as responsible about it when I was your age. I guess because my whole family was here and we were all traveling, it seemed quite normal. But when you think about it, it's not normal at all! It's truly exceptional. I may take it for granted on occasion. To be honest, I was so happy when I was able to travel by myself that I never stopped to question how it was even possible to do so," she concluded.

"I can't wait to get to a point where this all seems normal and ho-hum! You've been so patient with me, Phyllis, and I can't thank you enough for everything. I'm so sorry I missed yoga and meditation these last two mornings. I enjoyed them and I'd like to make it a habit, at least on weekdays. I like routines, they keep me grounded." She gave her aunt a long hug and a kiss on the cheek. "So, if I want to get up on time, I need to hit the sack!" added Lola as she stifled a yawn.

"I'm tired too. I'll walk up with you," responded Phyllis as she closed the glass fireplace gates and switched off the light.

CHAPTER 32
DAD

LOLA WAS QUITE pleased with herself for getting up on time to start the day the way she wanted to. She enjoyed those quiet moments with her aunt, especially when they did it outside in the gazebo. She liked hearing the birds and feeling the breeze in her hair, though she imagined she wasn't supposed to be noticing those if she was meditating! No matter what, it felt good.

After breakfast, she even went for a walk on her own. She was trying not to think about anything in particular. That was her new resolution, no overthinking. Just enjoying the moment. She heard a sort of thwack behind her and turned, thinking it was an animal, but to her utter bewilderment, a door opened in midair, and out came a man, dressed in khakis with an Indiana Jones type of hat. She stood there dumbfounded as the man looked around and finally settled his eyes on her.

"Oh, hello, darling. It looks like I'm right on time! I've been trying to get you alone for days now," he said with a wide grin.

"Uuuuh......" she stammered, completely dumbstruck.

"I'm sorry, love, it's me, Simon, your father!"

Lola promptly fell to the floor, unconscious.

She came to a few moments later when someone was lightly tapping her hand.

"Oh, thank God. I was hoping I wouldn't have to go and get someone to rouse you. This is complicated enough," said the man.

Lola stared at him wide-eyed and scrambled to sit up. "Dad! Is that really you?" she squeaked out, looking around her to see if perhaps this was a dream, or worse, if some lunatic was pretending to be her dad, back from the dead. She had to get a grip and focus!

"Yes, love, it's me. I'm so happy to see you all grown up. And I'm sorry for the theatrics. I didn't mean to frighten you." Simon was wringing his hands, looking genuinely worried.

"You scared the shit out of me!" blurted Lola. She was staring at him intently, and sure enough, he looked like her father. "Oh, sorry, I didn't mean to say it like that. I mean, I'm surprised. Though I did hope to figure out the whole-time travel thing eventually, I was not expecting this at all," she babbled.

"I see you got my letter. Have you settled in alright? Not too much of a culture shock? I know this is not the same lifestyle you were used to with your mom......" Simon trailed off. He seemed to be alluding to the Estate, more than the whole magic key traveling thing.

"Thanks for the letter and the locket. It's beautiful." He helped her up and seemed to hesitate about whether or not to give her a hug. He settled on brushing invisible grass from her back. Lola felt awkward and nervous. "Have you been to see Phyllis?" she asked.

"Oh, I see Phyllis all the time!" he responded with a smile and a dismissive wave.

"I mean, have you spoken to her yet?" Lola's voice trailed off in confusion, then anger as she realized her aunt had lied to her.

"Yes, only just. She filled me in on what you've been told so far. As far as we know, I'm the only one who's traveled ahead in time. Otherwise, we'd have met some of our ancestors." He suggested they walk further down the path, then remembered there was something she needed to know. "I don't think this had been made clear to you, but you can only travel from here to somewhere and from there back to here. You can't go from Paris to Rome, for example. That means if anyone else was jumping through time, they'd have to do it from here to here," he explained. "Of course, someone might have attempted it and stayed out of sight to avoid any negative consequences." He added, "Which is pretty much how I started out."

Lola drank in his face. This was such a precious opportunity. "How long can you stay?" she said quickly. "I have so many questions!"

"I have all the time in the world, love. But I think we should meet somewhere more private. Can you meet me in the schoolroom at 10 a.m.?"

"Yes, that's in about thirty minutes," said Lola looking at her watch. "Should I get Phyllis to join us?"

"No, this is just for the two of us to catch up. But we will need a strategy session with Phyllis sooner rather than later," Simon said ruefully.

"Okay, sounds good. See you later."

He took the key out of his pocket, and the door appeared. He turned back to her and waved before going through the door and disappearing.

Lola sank to the ground and exhaled. This was incredible! Her father, dead for over thirteen years, had just dropped in on her morning walk, not as a ghost, but as a time traveler. She wondered *when* he came from and how old she was in that timeline. Oh, this was giving her a headache. She still couldn't get used to it. Now she understood why they needed extra security on the grounds. And she was pretty sure that Jackson knew. If her dad had been popping in and out for years, Jackson would have caught him on camera at some point. Though why he wouldn't have discussed it with Phyllis was a mystery to Lola. Or perhaps he had, and they'd kept Lola in the dark. This was getting confusing and a bit insulting if she'd been excluded from the joke the whole time. But she didn't have time for a tantrum just then. She had to get to the schoolroom where, she hoped, all would be revealed.

She stopped in to let Phyllis know she'd be in the schoolroom with her dad and that she'd like to discuss it with her at some point during the day. They agreed to have lunch on Phyllis' balcony for privacy.

Lola then went to the schoolroom to wait for her dad. She was flipping through a chemistry book when he knocked on the outer door.

"I figured this was easier on the nerves than having a door appear out of nowhere," he said. He approached her tentatively and stopped about a foot away.

"Yes, thank you. I know you can't be circulating in the hall since Jackson or Marie, or even guests could see you," responded Lola, awkwardly.

"There are guests in the house?" he asked worriedly.

"No, not now. But my friend Jane will be here on Thursday night until Monday morning," said Lola. She was nervous. She could see he was waiting, gauging her reaction.

Simon smiled and said, "Ah yes, I remember Jane!" Simon didn't seem to know what to do with his hands. He kept reaching out to embrace her or stroke her hair but would just let them drop.

"You do?" asked Lola in disbelief.

"Yes, of course! I've been keeping tabs on you, love," said Simon with what he hoped was a loving smile.

"But how are you doing this? Aren't you sick?"

"It seems I'm not sick when I travel, only when I stay within my lifespan. So, I can no longer go back in time before I died, but I can travel further if that makes any sense," he said, relaxing a bit.

"Oh, so you know what's going to happen to me?" said Lola excitedly.

"Well, only a few things. It seems I can only travel up to your 16th birthday," he said sadly.

"But that's on Saturday!" exclaimed Lola.

"I know, we don't have a lot of time. I think the only reason I can travel through time at all is to pass along important information to you as my heir. Having Phyllis as Custodian isn't customary, and she doesn't know everything that needs to be passed along. So, I'm afraid our talks will need to be practical," said Simon apologetically.

"Maybe you could write some more letters to me? Or record yourself on my phone?" pleaded Lola.

"I'd love to, darling, but I'm afraid that's leaving too much evidence," Simon added. This was an untenable situation.

"I understand," Lola said with a sigh. She wished they had more time. She looked up at him, trying to convey her sorrow. He looked deep into her eyes and, as though communicating telepathically, they both got up and hugged, holding on for what seemed like a long time. When they finally broke apart, Simon asked in a choked-up voice, "Alright, let's hear those questions."

They went over basic traveling information and the responsibilities of the Custodian. They had a look at the Archives that Simon had asked Phyllis to hide in the schoolroom, and Simon answered a few other fundamental questions about their legacy. When Lola asked about his illness, her mother, and Jackson's parents, Simon also agreed that theirs had been an unfortunate fate and that there was a very real possibility that they had met early ends because they had not followed the plan. Lola asked what Simon thought of Jackson, of their unofficial betrothal and the likelihood of their marriage. Simon had always liked Jackson and had been keeping tabs on the boy for this purpose exactly. He was very much on board with Jackson as her prospective husband and confirmed that Jackson most likely knew about the traveling, though he could probably not explain it. It had never been discussed with Phyllis as far as he knew, but he figured it couldn't hurt for Lola to have an exploratory chat with Jackson to see what he'd pieced together and to have a little Q&A session with him.

It felt good to have been able to have this chat with her dad. She felt more confident about her place in the world and her upcoming duties and responsibilities. She also felt lighter, like she could start to enjoy her new life. It was too bad she couldn't bring Jackson with her through the door, but at least she might be able to talk to him about it before they had to get married. Two years was a long time to keep something as big as this a secret from someone you saw every day.

After a while, another question came to Lola. She asked if Simon knew of other families that had doors in their homes since they certainly couldn't be the only ones in the world. Simon said he'd been investigating that for years, but without the ability to go back in time or go out in public locally, he hadn't found much. Simon had tried many of the major libraries around the world and even talked to a few historians, but he could never give them any contact information to get back to him other than the addresses of their apartments. And well, people don't send snail mail anymore. In the end, he'd tasked the attorneys just before he died, hoping they would have an answer by the time Lola took over.

He was hoping Lola would be interested in doing some research on the matter. Perhaps at the local library or even online. He could give her the names of the people he'd been in contact with, and they could email her with information. It had to sound like academic research. Otherwise, people would get suspicious. Lola told him she had already started researching; besides, she was fascinated with the topic. Then it occurred to her that she could tell him her recent whereabouts and they could meet earlier than today. But would she remember today's conversation? Simon said that he would, but she wouldn't. It was a bit confusing, so they decided just to stick with their current plan. They agreed to meet after breakfast and after lunch every day until her birthday and just enjoy the time they had.

CHAPTER 33
SURPRISE

IT WAS ALREADY lunchtime when she went back to her room, so instead of going down to the dining room, she knocked on Phyllis' door to see if she was there. She was, and lunch had already been set up on the terrace. They had a nice chat about her visit with her dad, about the secrets and the confusing issues, and the sad reality that his visits would soon come to an end.

Phyllis tried words of comfort, "I was sad too at first, but now I have you to keep me company and share secrets with. And once your party and the 4th of July have passed, we'll have more time to travel together and enjoy it. I know it seems like a burden right now, but it is quite a lot of fun!"

They had lunch and talked about boys in general and Jackson in particular. Phyllis thought there was indeed something special about him. They also spoke more about Phyllis' life and the one who got away. She had met him in Moscow while on one of her travels, and after only spending a few days together, he proposed. At the time, it wasn't safe yet for Phyllis to travel in the usual manner, and besides, it would have meant moving to Moscow and leaving Simon alone. It just wasn't meant to be. Phyllis sadly remarked that she had never had that spark with anyone else. Lola tried to be positive and said that she was still young and could easily meet someone in the next few years. Now that Lola was preparing to take over as Custodian, Phyllis would be free to live life as she chose, with whomever she chose. And besides, Lola was sure whoever she met would love to live in their mansion. If there was a plan for the rest of them, there was certainly a plan for her too. Lola wanted her aunt to be happy.

After lunch, she went back to the schoolroom. Simon was already there, poring over the Archives. They went over the book, cover to cover, so Lola would have a good idea of its contents. They searched for mentions of other keys but could find none. Lola wondered if perhaps the lawyers would know as they seemed to have a part to play in this, which Simon responded to enthusiastically. She also asked if they were aware that he was traveling beyond the grave, and Simon said if they did, they hadn't said anything to him about it, nor to Phyllis. Surely his key would have been revoked if he was doing something wrong? Then they wondered if there might be a spell of some kind to call on elders or someone who might know. They searched the book for that as well but with no luck.

"What would happen if someone who wasn't an Evers had the key and knew how to use it? Do you think it would open and let them travel?" pondered Lola.

"I was told only someone from the Evers bloodline can use one of the keys. Also, I think there is something special about our own personal key. Like it might be calibrated just for us. I'm sure every one of us wondered about it but was too frightened of the possible consequences to ever try it," he explained.

Lola was quiet for a while and then said, "This might be off topic, but what about the caretaker situation? Shouldn't a couple be living here as caretakers? If Jackson and I get married, he can't stay on as the groundskeeper. I can barely stand to have him do it now. It feels weird. When I finished high school, we talked about enrolling in distance college classes together. He'll need time to study." Lola was pacing as she talked. It was so rewarding to have her dad there to bounce ideas off.

"I was thinking about that. I think you should ask the attorneys to look for a new couple. That way you don't have to worry about it. If you're sure about Jackson, then replacing him is what's best. However, if you're not, then we don't want to take away a job he's good at and enjoys," cautioned Simon.

"But he's still taking care of the accounts for Phyllis. And if he'd accepted Phyllis' offer to send him away to college, she'd have hired another couple anyway," countered Lola.

Simon snapped his fingers. "That's right. He'd be done by now and could just as easily have come back here to work in any other position, but not as the caretaker. He would then be on an equal footing as those other boys on the list of matches. Not that I care about that, but maybe the good people of Williamsburg do. I think that Jackson is worthy of you and a position in the Evers family regardless of whether he gets an Ivy League Education or not. What do you think?"

"I agree, and so does Phyllis, I'm sure. But I think he would feel better about it if he got your blessing. How do you feel about an accidental ghostly appearance tonight after dinner?" asked Lola.

"Sounds tricky, but I think you're right. He needs to be on board with us. Your mother and I messed things up, and I'd like to make it up to you and the family as best I can. And I think our ancestors would agree." Simon was nodding, mostly to himself.

"Okay, that's settled. I'll ask him to go for a walk after dinner. How does 8 p.m. sound? We'll be on the path somewhere near where you met me this morning." Lola was looking excited. Though Simon and Jackson already knew each other, it felt good to get them together as they were both very important to her.

"Perfect, darling, I'll see you then. Now go out and enjoy the rest of your day. You can't be cooped up in here all day with your old man!" chided Simon, pushing a strand of Lola's hair behind her ear.

"I love spending time with you. How about we meet in your room tomorrow so you can tell me about your paintings?" suggested Lola.

"Yes, of course!" replied Simon.

He gave her a long, tight hug, and then he left. She waited a bit and then went to her room to change into a swimsuit. A few hours by the pool would do her good.

JACKSON WASN'T AT DINNER, so Phyllis and Lola spent some quiet time together. When Marie left for the day, Lola broached the subject of having the attorneys find a new couple to ask as full-time caretakers. Seeing this was a serious topic, Phyllis put down her knife and fork and gave Lola her full attention. Encouraged, Lola added that she was likely to get her license and finish high school by December if she was doing it on her own. That way, both she and Jackson could start college after the holidays. Which meant there was still plenty of time for Lola to learn all the other skills she required, such as dancing and various etiquette lessons. Furthermore, Jackson could be her escort to most of her social events. Just because they had to wait until she was eighteen to wed didn't mean they couldn't get engaged in the next couple of years. Phyllis was impressed by Lola's planning and wondered if Lola would broach the subject with Jackson.

"Dad is going to do it," explained Lola.

"Come again?" The look on Phyllis' face was priceless.

"Dad is going to meet us tonight on the grounds, and he and Jackson are going to have a man-to-man chat. I thought it would be best for him to do it. Jackson's dad is gone, and he's got no one to counsel him. If Dad gives him his blessing, then he might feel better about letting go of the job and embracing his position as my future husband. I mean, I know he wants to, he has been very respectful of me and encouraged me to consider other boys. But I know it's him. I feel it in my bones. Whether that's part of the spell or not is pointless because that's what's going to happen anyway. We might as well embrace it and enjoy it. I mean, we could go away to college if we wanted to. It's just three years, and we'd come home on weekends so you wouldn't be alone. And you'd have the new caretakers with you," Lola added quickly.

"Oh, darling, don't worry about me!" Phyllis declared. "You do what is best for you."

"I'm not planning on leaving. But if Jackson wants to go, he should feel free to do so. We've got plenty of time for weddings and babies!" affirmed Lola, even as a blush crept up her neck.

"You're right, of course. I'll call the attorneys in the morning and suggest it." Phyllis seemed pleased with the development. She resumed eating, as did Lola, when another thought occurred to her.

"Oh, and ask them if they know of any other families who have a legacy similar to our own, or if they know of other books we could look into, to find out."

Phyllis clapped her hands together. "Brilliant, why didn't I ever think of that?"

Lola winked and said, "Two or three heads are better than one! Anyway, I should go find Jackson. Otherwise, my plan won't work."

"Okay, darling, come to say goodnight if it's not too late," replied Phyllis.

"Sure thing," answered Lola.

Lola walked over to the garage. The door was open, and there was music streaming loudly. To avoid a repeat performance, she texted Jackson from the door opening. As anticipated, he reached into his jeans and got the phone out, then his head came up and around from under the hood. He smiled and put the phone back into his pocket, and wiped his hands on a rag as he walked towards her.

"Hey, gorgeous! To what do I owe this lovely visit?" He leaned against the wall casually, thumbs in his pockets.

"I thought we might go for a walk," suggested Lola. "I missed you at dinner," she added shyly.

"Well, I can't eat at your place every night," said Jackson laughing.

He didn't seem to be making fun of her, so she added, "I know, but I still missed you."

Jackson's smile widened, and he straightened up. "I missed you too, and I'm glad you came over. Let me just change into cleaner clothes."

He gave her a peck on the cheek and went up to his apartment. It was 7:45 p.m. when he came back down. Perfect timing. They headed towards the path, and Jackson took her hand. She was hoping he would kiss her again but a little nervous that he would do it at the exact moment her dad would appear. That would be embarrassing. *Oh my god, what if Dad has already seen us kissing when he was keeping tabs on me? What if that's what he meant about finally getting me alone? How mortifying!*

"*Now,* what are you thinking about? You've got that serious, worried look," asked Jackson, frowning at her.

"Oh, nothing. It's a little hard to explain," said Lola with a pained expression.

"A lady of mystery, I like it!" Jackson gave her a nudge with an elbow and resumed holding her hand.

"I have a question for you," said Lola, steering the conversation in the direction she needed it to go.

"Shoot!" said Jackson in a casual manner, breathing in the evening air.

"What other types of unusual activity have you recorded with the new sophisticated security system?" said Lola carefully.

Jackson looked puzzled. "What do you mean?"

Lola kept her eyes ahead of her to avoid looking guilty or suspicious. "Well, you said it was mostly animals, but have you spotted anything else?" she inquired.

Jackson seemed to take the question in stride and answered, "An intruder or two."

"Did you ever catch them or only saw them on camera?" continued Lola.

"Only on camera," was Jackson's response.

And the final leading question. "Did you recognize anyone?" It came out almost a whisper.

Jackson stopped walking and placed his hands on her shoulders. "Where are you heading with these questions, Lola?"

Just then, there was a rustling in the bushes behind them, and Lola yelped.

"I think she's asking if you ever saw *me* on camera," said Simon as calmly as he could.

Jackson gasped and took a step back, hands up in a defensive pose. He blinked a few times, looking back and forth between the man and a beaming Lola, and exclaimed, "Jesus Christ, Mr. Evers! Is that you?"

"In the flesh. I mean that literally. I'm not a ghost or anything," Simon specified.

"But-but you're dead." Jackson had gone so pale it looked as if he was the ghost.

Simon chuckled, amused at this turn of events. "Yes, I am. Why don't you walk Lola back to the house, and you and I can have a chat, son?"

Jackson was trying to regain his composure. "Um...okay. You'll be here when I get back?" he asked.

"I think I'll wait for you in the pool house. It'll be more comfortable for both of us," answered Simon.

Lola took Jackson's hand and led them back to the house. He seemed uncomfortable about it and kept looking back towards Simon.

"Don't worry about it. He knows about us," said Lola reassuringly.

"What does he know? What has he seen?" Jackson asked in a panic.

"Nothing untoward obviously. You've been nothing but a gentleman since we've met," quipped Lola.

"I know, but it's feeling a little creepy right about now." Jackson was looking a little nauseated.

"I know. I got the same feeling the first time I saw him," Lola reassured him.

When they got to the house, Jackson demanded, "What's going on, Lola?"

"I thought maybe you knew?" she said soothingly.

"Knew what?" asked Jackson, flabbergasted. "That your dad didn't die?" he said a little too loudly.

Lola looked around her and shushed him. "He did die. I just meant you might have seen him on your cameras and wondered," whispered Lola.

Jackson was looking at her like she was insane. He probably thought this made no sense. But then, somehow, it did. "You are making no sense at all. I thought I had seen him once or twice but figured it was my imagination playing tricks on me or having one too many beers with my friends," he admitted.

"You drink beer?" teased Lola. "You have friends?" she added, trying to lighten the mood.

"That's not the point!" snapped Jackson. He was obviously having none of her jokes.

"My dad will explain everything. Come see me when you're done. I'll be in the library with Phyllis. You might need something stronger than beer by that time," said Lola gravely.

"What!?" Jackson exclaimed. This was not going well at all. Hopefully, Simon was better at this than she was.

"Never mind, just go," she said with a light shove.

He saw her safely into the house and made his way to the pool house. He was gone for over two hours, and, in that time, Lola had fallen asleep on the window seat in the library, and Phyllis had gone to bed.

WHEN HE CAME BACK, he stroked her hair and spoke her name softly.

"I'm sorry it's so late. I had a lot of questions," he whispered.

"It's okay. I had a lot of questions, too!" said Lola sleepily.

"Shall I carry you up to bed?" he suggested hopefully.

Lola blushed and sat up quickly. "I'm awake, I can manage, but you could walk me up to my room if you want." She was fussing with her hair and checking if she had drooled or something during her little nap.

Jackson took in her mussed appearance and tucked a strand of hair behind her ear. "Just to the sitting room, no further!" he warned, wagging a finger at her like she was a naughty child.

Lola put on a mock pout and responded, "Spoilsport!"

He walked her to her room but declined her invitation to go in. He obviously needed time to process all this information before he was ready to talk about it. He suggested they meet after dinner and spend the following evening together. He took her hands, looked into the hall on either side, and kissed her on the lips. It was a quick kiss, but she still enjoyed it and sighed against his lips. She could tell he was worried that Simon was watching them. He smiled and said goodnight.

CHAPTER 34
STUDIO

THE FOLLOWING MORNING AT BREAKFAST, after meditation and yoga, Phyllis announced they were dining at the Borden's. She asked if the invitation should be extended to Jackson, but Lola thought it would be rude to add an extra person at the last minute. Besides, she assumed it was another family bent on matchmaking, and they would surely not appreciate Lola arriving with an escort. Furthermore, Lola thought to herself, it was really hard to consider prospective matches when Jackson was around because she was so keenly aware of him, and it was distracting.

Phyllis gave her a rundown of what to expect and what she might consider wearing. Lola asked if Jackson already knew about the plans to which Phyllis replied yes. Phyllis advised Lola that they would leave around 5 p.m. and should meet in the foyer and that she would be out most of the day.

Lola quickly texted Jackson to ask him to have lunch with her instead of meeting after dinner. If there was time, maybe they could take a dip in the pool after she'd be done with her dad. He agreed but suggested she have Marie pack a picnic basket for them instead so they could eat outside in the gazebo and have a little more privacy for their chat.

Then, she ran to her room to get dressed and knocked on her dad's door promptly at 10 a.m.

Knowing that he could obviously not answer the door since he was supposed to be deceased, she went in and headed for the alcove studio. He was already there and was working on a portrait of her mother. It hadn't been there the other day.

"She's beautiful!" gushed Lola. "She looks so young. I guess she was when you met her and when last you saw her."

"I was really sad to hear she passed away and upset that both your parents were taken from you at such a young age."

"I'll always miss her, but it's getting easier to cope with it. It wasn't easy seeing her so sick and, well, helpless. She was always so competent and efficient. The good news was that it didn't last long. She was gone in a matter of months. Was it like that for you?" asked Lola, wondering if this was a sore subject.

"My death didn't come quickly. I battled cancer for two years before my body finally gave up on me. I think it might have gone faster if I hadn't traveled as much," said Simon with regret. He gestured toward some chairs in the corner of the room, and they sat.

Lola looked thoughtful. "Is that where you came from? The time when you were first diagnosed?" she asked.

"Yes. It's a good thing there was just me and Phyllis in the house because it's very confusing going back and forth. This morning, you were three years old in my time, and your mother was angry with me and wouldn't take my calls. She would send pictures every few months with a quick note on how you were doing. Now, here you are, all grown up, and your mother is gone. I hate leaving you, so I just stay here during the days and go back at night.

"So, in truth, the cancer has barely had time to progress. I've given up trying to imagine what would have happened if I had done things differently. The truth is, I loved your mother, and she gave me you. I don't regret that." Simon took her hand and squeezed it.

"I know. And I may have been upset I didn't have a father growing up, but I think things turned out okay in the end. I have a nice home, an aunt who loves me, and I get to spend some time getting to know you," said Lola gratefully.

They talked some more, and he showed her his other paintings. He had done quite a few of Lola as she was growing up, and they were all lovely. He suggested they have some of them hung in the mansion. Lola was too self-conscious to agree to that and said he should talk to Phyllis about any decorating changes he had in mind. He gave her a few painting lessons, and Lola tried her hand at reproducing a bowl of fake fruit. She was terrible!

She left her father to go have lunch with Jackson, and they promised to meet back there at 2 p.m.

CHAPTER 35
PICNIC

WHEN SHE GOT to the gazebo, Jackson was nowhere to be found. Neither was the picnic basket. She went out by the pool in case they got their signals crossed but found it empty as well. As she was wondering if perhaps, she should go back to the house and look for both the basket and Jackson, she heard him whistle. She followed the sound to the lawn beyond the pool. Jackson had set up a blanket and laid out the food. He explained it would do her good to be out in the sun instead of under the gazebo. When she joined him, he handed her a glass of sweet tea.

Jackson jumped straight into the main topic. "So, you've just found out about all of this in the last week?" he asked incredulously.

Lola nodded. "Yes, it completely blew my mind. I was about to have an aneurism. I'm so glad I can talk to you about it. Normally, we can't talk about it with anyone outside of the family." Lola visibly relaxed. She took a plate and started loading it with some cheese, crackers, olives, and finger sandwiches.

Jackson seemed pleased to be included, but still, he asked, "Why make an exception now?" He too took a plate and chose a selection of goodies.

"Didn't you discuss this with my dad yesterday?" asked Lola. She should have asked Simon for a rundown of the conversation.

Jackson popped some grapes in his mouth and replied, "I did, but I want your take on it." He continued to eat like this was just an everyday topic of conversation.

Lola stopped eating. She was feeling self-conscious. "Well, you know," said Lola hesitantly.

Jackson looked at her intently and said, "No, tell me."

Lola's face was bright red when she said, "I like you."

"I like you too!" he said matter-of-factly.

Lola gave his shoulder a little shove and said, "I mean, I *like* you."

Jackson returned the shove and said, "I *like* you too."

Great! This was Grade 2 all over again. "Oh God, you're going to have me spell it out for you, aren't you?" said Lola in irritation.

"A man never asks an important question he doesn't already know the answer to," said Jackson, somewhat cryptically.

Lola looked at Jackson in confusion—boys were unbelievable! "What are you talking about?" she cried in confusion.

Jackson looked at her patiently, took her hands, and said, "Before I propose to you, I want to make sure you are going to say yes, and that you are going to say yes for the right reasons." He sat there expectantly, letting that sink in.

Lola's jaw dropped. "Holy shit, are you going to propose *today*? Is that what the picnic was for?" shrieked Lola, her eyes wide with panic.

"Of course not, and from that reaction, it's not the right time anyway!" barked Jackson. "Like I'd have you ask Marie to pack a picnic. What kind of amateur do you think I am?" he said in a huff. He got up and started pacing back and forth.

Lola placed her hands on her head and put her forehead on the blanket. "My head hurts."

Jackson stopped and took a deep breath. "Let's start over. Lola, I like you, and you like me. If and when I do propose, would you accept? And would you accept because you want to be with me for the rest of your life, or is there another reason why you would accept? Or, God forbid, refuse?" He sank to his knees beside her and raised her chin so she would look at him.

Lola bit her lip as if thinking. "I do like you, a lot, more than anyone else I've met so far. And I would never refuse, though there are other reasons why I would accept. I think you're handsome and I like it when you kiss me. I think you're smart, and I feel safe and cared for by you. We've only just met, but you already feel like you're my best friend, and I can count on you. And there is also the whole fate thing. Does that answer your question? What about you? Why would you want to marry me?" she asked.

He sat down. "This could take a while!" he said with a laugh, and Lola began to relax. "Firstly, you are the most beautiful, natural girl I've ever met. You are smart and funny and completely in need of someone to take care of you and keep you grounded. That would be me. You are caring and generous, and you don't judge people." He let that sink in.

"You've only just met me. How could you know all that about me?" protested Lola.

Jackson waited for a beat and said, "I've been watching you."

"That doesn't sound creepy at all......" said Lola, rolling her eyes.

Jackson retrieved Lola's plate and gently urged her to resume eating. He took his own and bit into a sandwich. "Stop that, you know what I mean. I pay attention when I'm around you. All this could have gone to your head, and it hasn't," he said.

"I don't think I've had time to fully absorb all of this. But the fact is, lots of people have arranged marriages, and they turn out fine. I figure we've got the basics covered. Anything else that comes up we'll learn to deal with together," said Lola. She was feeling better and realized she was famished.

"My sentiments exactly," agreed Jackson. "But just to be clear, I'm not going to propose any time soon. It's too soon, you're too young, and you should make some friends in the area. I don't want us to be joined at the hip forevermore." They were both done with lunch, so he took out the peach cobbler Marie had packed for dessert and the thermos of coffee. He served them both a bowl while Lola poured out two cups.

"That means you won't be escorting me to all my events?" Lola said between mouthfuls of cobbler.

"We'll take it week by week, see what Phyllis thinks. I still have to drive you to most of them anyway, so unless someone asks you out, I can still be your escort. But if we're always seen together, people will pair us in their minds, and you won't be invited to as many events," said Jackson.

"Is that a bad thing? Dances and dinner parties aren't my ideas of fun," moaned Lola.

Jackson shook his head. "I know, but if we're meant to become influential members of society, we need to circulate in society. And you, my dear, need a coming-out party before that can even be considered," he said, polishing off his cobbler and reaching for another serving.

Lola laughed. "Are you kidding? I thought that was a joke!" When Jackson kept a straight face, Lola started to panic again.

"You can ask Phyllis how funny it is," said Jackson somberly.

She would broach the topic with Phyllis. Coming out, indeed!

"Fine. But then instead of inviting single guys to dinner, we should be inviting girls my age so I can make friends, as you said. That seems to be a better use of my time," Lola said petulantly. She finished her cobbler and held her plate in the air expectantly. Jackson laughed and served her another piece.

"You'll need both. But don't worry. Your coming-out party will likely be disguised as your sweet sixteen birthday party this weekend. I mailed the invitations yesterday. Phyllis invited a ton of people," he added.

Lola exhaled noisily. "That's Saturday night?" she asked anxiously.

"Yes, anyone who's anyone will be here. And it's actually at 4 p.m. It's a garden party, and it's also to celebrate the 4th of July. That should take some of the heat off of you. Besides, Saturday is also Phyllis' birthday," added Jackson.

"That's right. Okay, I feel better about it," said Lola, relaxing again.

Since they were both done eating, they packed up the leftovers and moved the basket so they could lie down on the blanket. Once they were settled, Jackson said, "Alright, so tell me about the key!"

They spent the rest of their lunch hour talking about where each of them would like to travel. Considering Lola's finances, they could go wherever they wanted, with or without the key. For safety, they agreed that she should phone him on his cell phone when she went somewhere. That way, if there was a problem, he could assist her. Unless, of course, she was in the middle of the rainforest! It was a lovely picnic, and Lola was happy that Jackson kissed her a few times. She liked it when he played with her hair or stroked her cheek. When he looked at her, she felt like he was looking at a rare and beautiful painting. And she liked looking at him too.

After lunch, Jackson went back to work, and Lola realized she knew very little about his daily schedule. She made a mental note to ask him later. She went to meet her father in his room for some more catching up and studying the Archives together. Simon had asked that she bring her laptop with her so she could surf the web as computers thirteen years ago weren't that interesting, and she was better at them than he was. Time flew quickly, and at 4 p.m., she had to call it a day so she could get ready to leave with Phyllis, but they promised to see each other the next day. She had a few days until Jane arrived. Then Lola would have to split her time between Simon, Phyllis, Jane, and Jackson. Now she knew why Phyllis took so many naps! Maybe she wasn't always traveling! Lola's days were long and full, and she dropped off like a light every night.

THE EVENING at the Bordens went well. She got along very well with their kids, Rory and Max, twins that were her age who promised to keep in touch. They had a beach house and hoped that Lola could come to stay for a while over the summer. She was able to practice her diplomatic response by saying her calendar was quite full until mid-July but would gladly come later in the month. That pleased them a lot as they said they would make a house party out of it and invite a bunch of other kids. When Lola seemed surprised, they said their *beach house* had ten bedrooms, one or two of which looked a lot like Lola's nursery and could accommodate a lot of guests. The invitation included Phyllis and Jackson, of course.

It seemed that people were pairing the two of them together even if he didn't escort her to every event. Maybe they had seen the way they looked at each other at the dance. No matter, it made things easier than having to pretend to like some of the boys. This way, they could all be friends.

Jackson picked them up around 11 p.m., and she could barely keep her eyes open when they got home. She hugged him goodnight, and he surprised her with a variation on his chaste kisses by kissing her temple this time.

Phyllis smiled as she observed the budding romance fondly and then retired for the night.

CHAPTER 36
MISSING

THE NEXT COUPLE of days were a blur. The days flew by, and Lola settled into a routine—in the morning, she would meditate, do yoga with Phyllis, then have breakfast with Jackson. The rest of the morning and lunchtime she spent with her dad. Most afternoons were spent napping, reading, and tanning by the pool. Jackson would usually pop by for a while when he could. Phyllis never made plans for them two nights in a row, so there was time to recuperate. *Thank God*, Lola thought!

Today, she didn't even read her book. Lola plopped onto one of the lounge chairs and fell asleep. By now, she was used to Jackson showing up. She didn't startle when someone stroked her hair and called her name. She just said, "Go away, I'm napping," and shooed him off like a fly.

"Lola, darling, it's me, Dad. You have to wake up," said Simon insistently.

"What? Dad, what are you doing here?" said Lola sleepily.

Simon was wringing his hands. "It's Phyllis. She's not in her room, and she promised to meet me there at 3 p.m. I need you to text her phone and find out where she is. I'm worried. I knocked repeatedly on her door, but she is not answering, and the door is locked. I don't know where she keeps her master key. Do you have one?" he asked anxiously.

"Right, yes, okay," agreed Lola getting up and reaching for her phone.

Lola texted Phyllis and got no response. She tried calling her as well, but she didn't pick up. Then she texted Jackson in case he had driven her somewhere, but he hadn't seen her all day. They went back to the house and went to the library to check on the calendar, and there were no events or tasks written in for today. She went to the kitchen to ask Marie if she'd seen Phyllis and was told that Phyllis went up to her room to rest after lunch.

"Was she ill?" asked Lola.

"No," replied Marie, "she just likes to rest in the afternoon." Nothing unusual as far as she was concerned.

Lola went up to her room to get her master key. She knocked, waited, then entered Phyllis' room. Phyllis wasn't there. She checked the bathroom, closet, and balcony, Simon trailing behind her, calling out to his sister. That, at least, ruled out any possibility of her collapsing in her room. Lola was starting to get worried. Phyllis usually told her if she would be traveling, and she'd made plans with Simon, so she should have been back by now. Since neither knew where she had disappeared to, it's not like they could follow her there using a key.

Lola snapped her fingers. "What if we used the key, and instead of focusing on a place, we just focused on Phyllis? Maybe the door would lead us there. What do you think?" she asked hopefully.

"I think it's worth a try. But if I do it, I fear it'll take me back home to the Phyllis of my timeline," said Simon with a pained expression.

"Then I should try it," suggested Lola.

"I don't know. It's a little risky. You don't have a lot of experience," warned Simon.

Lola put a hand on Simon's arm soothingly and said, "I worked out a system with Jackson where I phone him when I get to the other side. The only problem is if it's in an area without cell service. Let me go get my key and change into some clothes."

Simon relaxed. "Yes, let's do that," he said, then, "Check the hall, and I'll go wait for you in the attic."

Lola checked the hall, and he made his way to the attic. When she got to her room, she texted Jackson, and he said he'd come to keep watch on the second floor and text her if Phyllis showed up. He would also check the grounds and all the rooms in the house, just in case, they had missed her.

Lola and Simon stood in front of the door. Simon asked if this was her first time, and she said no, but had only conjured one door so far by herself. He suggested she practice one more time, just to get comfortable. Lola took a deep breath, put the key in the lock, and thought of the path on the Estate. As she turned the lock, the door opened up, and there was the path. It was that easy!

She closed the door and took another deep breath, and focused on Phyllis the way she had looked at breakfast with her ivory skirt and her flowery top, her hair in a loose bun with tendrils curling up around her face. She avoided imagining her at a specific location so as not to end up in the breakfast room. She turned the key and opened the door. She had no idea where the door led, but she went through with Simon following close behind. It was dark, but it was obvious they were in some kind of fancy park or garden. "Do you know where we are?" she asked expectantly. Simon clapped his hands and beamed. "Florence!" he exclaimed. "Specifically, in the Giardino Bardani," he added.

Impressed, Lola asked, "How do you know?"

Simon smiled and replied, "We used to come here all the time with our parents as kids. Even in the dark, I'd know it from anywhere else in the world, just by the smell of the wisteria."

They texted Jackson where they were and, as they had an apartment in the city, said they would call as soon as they made it there or found Phyllis. Then, Simon asked if Jackson could get them a cab to pick them up in front of the Porta San Giorgio in fifteen minutes since that would go faster. They walked the paths of the darkened gardens. As they passed through the famous Wisteria Arbor, Lola was able to smell the wisteria even if she could not see their vivid purple hue.

With the time difference, it was about 10 p.m. in Florence, so there was no chance of them being seen unless they had surveillance cameras.

When they go to the end of the path they were on, they hit a wall. Literally. "Dad, I don't think we can get over that," said Lola in a panic.

"Don't worry, we'll just cut through these bushes. See, it's someone's backyard. They don't have a fence, and we will reach the street in no time," was Simon's reply.

She was hoping these people didn't have surveillance cameras, or worse, a huge dog waiting for them. She followed Simon, and sure enough, they made it to the street and could see the cab waiting near the Porta San Giorgio.

It was a huge brick arch with two giant doors which, she would learn on the cab ride, was the gate or portal of the former outer medieval walls of the city of Verona, Italy. Simon gave the address of the apartment to the driver, and they were off. Lola couldn't believe she was in Italy!

It took no longer than ten minutes to get to the Piazza Giuseppe Poggi, right next to the Poggi Tower. Jackson had already paid the driver by credit card, but Lola wondered how they were going to get into the apartment without a key. Turns out it wasn't a multi-story building, but more of a townhouse. There was a gate with a code, then down a few steps to the door where a lockbox was around the door handle. Simon punched in the code on the keypad, and a hatch opened so he could access the key. How clever! They rang the bell, just in case, but got no response. It was a second-floor walk-up. When they got to the top of the stairs, another door waited, but this one was not locked. They called out for Phyllis and went room to room, just in case.

There was no evidence of Phyllis having been there at all. Lola could tell Simon was even more worried than she was. Why would the door bring them to Florence if Phyllis wasn't here? He went to the safe and took out some money and the cell phone. Once he had it charging, he had Lola call Jackson to let him know they had arrived safely and see if he'd had any luck on his end. Jackson had searched the house and the grounds and found no trace of Phyllis. He had located her cell phone; it was still in her room.

Simon called a few of the restaurants in town that Phyllis liked, but none of them had seen her. Simon asked if Lola wanted to grab a bite to eat, but she didn't want to leave in case Phyllis came back. Simon went to the pantry where a few shelf-stable items were stored. They managed to put together a dinner of *Pane carasau,* a traditional flatbread from Sardinia, porcini mushrooms from a jar, olive paste from a tube, and truffles in a cream sauce. For dessert, they found Panettone in a tin which they paired with the most delicious Espresso Lola had ever had. Granted, Lola had never had Espresso, but it was still the best.

After dinner, Simon gave her the tour of the place, wrote down the codes to get back in the apartment should she go out, and gave her the money he had taken out of the safe. He had to get back home, or the Phyllis in his timeline would worry. He'd poke around and ask what her favorite places were in Florence.

"Will you be okay here, alone?" he asked. "Try to get some sleep. I'll be back as soon as I can." Since he needed to go back from the attic, Lola took out her key and opened the door for him. They hugged good night, and he was gone.

After Simon left, she called Jackson, and he tried to reassure her everything was going to be alright. She should take a hot shower and get some sleep. Lola found some toiletries in the bathroom and borrowed one of Phyllis' nightgowns to wear after her shower. She felt better. Though it was now 2 a.m. here in Florence, on Lola's watch, it was only 8 p.m. Despite the fact that she was exhausted, she was still too keyed up to sleep. Maybe the Espresso wasn't such a good idea. Lola thought about the layout of the apartment and remembered that there was a mini library nook. She went over, hoping the books were not all in Italian. Lo and behold, they had an English copy of *The Great Gatsby*. Lola went to the bedroom, got in under the covers, and opened to the place where she had left off on the other side.

CHAPTER 37
FLORENCE

SHE WOKE to the sound of someone pounding on the front door. Checking the clock, she saw it was 10 a.m.; she'd slept like the dead. She went to the door and peered out the peephole to see who it was, expecting either her dad or Phyllis. But it was Jackson! She quickly unlocked the door and let him in, mouth hanging open in disbelief. He was carrying two coffees and a bag of what smelled like pastries. Her mouth immediately started watering.

"What are you doing here?" she said excitedly. "How did you get here?"

He gave her a peck on the cheek and walked to the kitchen counter to set down his things. Lola was following so close behind that she ran into his back when he stopped.

"Good morning to you too! Is it me or the coffee you are so excited about?" he asked with a chuckle. Then he took in her appearance, and his smile widened as he nodded appreciatively.

Lola saw the look and realized she was essentially wearing a negligee. She shrieked and ran from the room. "Back in a minute," she called out as she went to look for a robe to put on. She found one behind the bathroom door and took a moment to brush her teeth and check her hair. She composed herself and went back into the kitchen.

Jackson had set his backpack on the ground and was sipping from one of the coffee cups. When he saw her, he pretended to pout at her tightly closed robe but didn't mention it. She was obviously embarrassed. Lola padded over, took the other cup, and said, "Now, explain!"

"Simon came back and said you hadn't found Phyllis. I hadn't found her either. He went back to his time to check in with his Phyllis. One of Phyllis' friends owns a jet and is always glad to help in an emergency. I just got off the plane," he explained.

Lola sat next to him on a stool at the counter, and they started digging into the pastries. "Oh my God, that's incredible! I've never even taken a plane, let alone a private jet! And you just flew clear across the country at a moment's notice. How did you even have time to pack?" Lola asked, mystified.

"I keep an overnight bag packed in case I need to stay over when driving Phyllis. It has the basics, and you'd be surprised what you can accomplish with a cell phone and a platinum card. I've been doing this for a while," said Jackson with a wink.

Lola was obviously impressed. She just stared at him. "You're so organized and worldly. I feel like a country bumpkin next to you!" she wailed.

"Lola, you haven't even finished high school. Give yourself a break. A year from now, you'll be as *worldly* as I am," he replied reassuringly. He kissed her forehead and got up to clear their breakfast. "Why don't you go home and change your clothes. I'll make some phone calls. I have Phyllis' credit card statements and can check her favorite stores to see if she's been there. I'll also check the cell phone records to see if she's used it recently," he added.

"Are you sure?" asked Lola. She knew she could borrow some of Phyllis' clothes, but they wouldn't fit right, and besides, someone needed to tell Marie they were out of the house so she wouldn't worry.

"Yes, don't worry about it," replied Jackson.

A sudden thought crossed Lola's mind. "What if I can't come back here?" asked Lola nervously.

"I assume you can just memorize the address and open the door into the apartment. That should be specific enough," he suggested, not exactly sure how the process worked.

"Good idea. Okay, here I go," she said, then paused. "Dad charged the cell phone and made some calls yesterday just so you don't think it was Phyllis."

Lola took out the key, and the door appeared. She thought of home, her new home, and the door opened to the attic stairs. She waved goodbye to an open-mouthed Jackson and promised to be back within the hour.

When she got home, she checked her aunt's room again. Still nothing. She checked the alarm clock—it was only 5 a.m.! This was so confusing! *It was mid-morning two minutes ago in Florence*, thought Lola.

She went to her room to shower and change. She grabbed a jacket and her passport in case she needed them later. Then she got a piece of paper and wrote Phyllis a note saying they were looking for her and where they had gone to. After checking the library, she went to the kitchen to leave a note for Marie. She wrote that she and Jackson had gone to the Florence apartment and to call them if Phyllis turned up, as Lola had not seen her aunt to let her know. She figured that would explain things a little.

Lola went to the attic stairs and hoped she'd get back to the Florence apartment with no problems.

It went well, and she even gave Jackson a start. He was remarkably level-headed about this whole door-travel thing and about her aunt's disappearance as well. Lola, however, thought she might need a Xanax before they made it to lunch.

"Any news?" he asked.

"Not really, but Simon traveled to the house in our time long enough to leave me a note saying he'd meet us here at noon so he could get some rest. He asked his Phyllis where she might have gone, and Phyllis suggested we look up Boris Ivanov. They had a fling when she was younger, and they met in Florence as he keeps a home here as well," explained Lola.

Jackson looked thoughtful. "My parents told me about it when I asked why she wasn't married. Apparently, it wasn't meant to be because she couldn't move to Russia to be with him. Maybe now that you're here, they might make a go of it. Wait, maybe that's what they did!" He brightened as he said it.

"Sure, that sounds romantic and all, but surely, she would have let us know she was staying a few days if that was the case. And she's known him a long time, so it's not like she got swept off her feet and lost track of time. No, I think something's gone wrong. Though contacting Ivanov could give us additional resources," replied Lola.

"Right, he's most likely her age and knows more about her than we do and would probably get more out the authorities than a couple of American teenagers," mused Jackson. "I'm on it," he added as he got up.

Jackson took a laptop out of his bag and started researching Boris Ivanov. He found a few listings, which he cross-referenced with the frequently called numbers in the phone records. It seems Boris and Phyllis had been in contact at least once a year for the last ten years. He dug into the credit card bills and found charges every year for the same hotel in Prague—the Four Seasons. He also found flight information from Florence to Prague around those same dates. They came to the conclusion that Phyllis would use the door to Florence, then fly to Prague to meet with Boris, or someone else, every year for a week, usually around her birthday.

"Maybe she came here to let him know that she couldn't make it this year because of me," suggested Lola.

"Right, but she could have called him. That would have been simpler," countered Jackson.

"Maybe he's married or a very influential man now, and it would look odd to have an American woman call him out of the blue," wondered Lola.

"Then it would make sense that she would come here to place the phone call. But then, wouldn't she just come right back? And for that matter, everyone has a cell phone now. He would have given her a private number to call if he was in a delicate situation," reasoned Jackson.

"Maybe he really wanted to see her, and she decided to pop in for a quick visit and got sidetracked. Maybe she can't use the key because she's always surrounded by people?" tried Lola.

"True," pondered Jackson. "But if she took a plane to Prague, we'd see it on the credit card statement."

"Maybe there wasn't time to warn him, and she went there directly," Lola said with a frown.

"That would be tricky. And why would the door lead us here?" asked Jackson, getting frustrated. He got up and started walking around the room.

Lola sighed and said, "She probably came here first, tried to call him, then seeing it was too late, went back and used a door to Prague."

"That makes sense, but it's only July 3. It's too early for the week in Prague. And there doesn't seem to be a reservation anyway. I don't see a charge unless they only charge the room after you've checked in. We should call the hotel to ask about the reservation," said Jackson.

He took out the phone, dialed the Four Seasons in Prague, and asked for Phyllis Evers. He was told Ms. Evers was not in residence and had canceled her reservation weeks ago, to which he thanked the man and hung up.

"That means she may have taken a door directly to Russia. But where? I think we'll need to call Boris," said Lola anxiously.

"You're right. I'll place the call, but I think it'll be better if you talk to him. He'll recognize the name," said Jackson, nodding.

"Alright, but I don't speak Russian!" exclaimed Lola.

"I'm sure he speaks English," Jackson said with a laugh.

"Oh right," Lola added sheepishly.

Jackson placed the call and asked for Boris Ivanov, saying that Ms. Lola Evers was calling from America. Lola had her fingers crossed, hoping he would take the call. They were put on hold for what seemed like an eternity, but then a man came on the line.

This is Boris Ivanov. How can I help you?

"Hello, Mr. Ivanov. My name is Lola Evers. I am Phyllis Evers' niece. I'm calling from Florence."

Hello, Ms. Evers.

"I'm very sorry to bother you, sir, but we are looking for my aunt. We can't seem to find her anywhere, and we thought she might be with you."

Oh. No, I'm afraid she isn't. We were meant to spend the week in Prague together for her birthday as we do every year, but she asked to postpone the trip this year because of your arrival. I have not spoken to her since we canceled the trip a few weeks ago.

"Oh. That's too bad. I'm really worried about her. We can't find her anywhere. She's not at home, she's not here in Florence, and no one has seen her."

Now, I'm worried. It's not like her to be mysterious. And she was looking forward to your visit and birthday party. Let me make some calls and get back to you.

"Thank you, sir. I truly appreciate it!"

Anything for Phyllis or those she loves. I'll ring you on this number?

"Yes, please. And thanks again."

"Don't mention it."

Lola relayed the information to Jackson, and they wondered what to do while they waited for Simon to arrive. Jackson said he'd call the other apartments and cell phones they owned in Europe in case she might have popped into one of those. He got no answer. They left a note for Simon in case he arrived early and went to buy food for lunch.

CHAPTER 38
SEARCHING

FLORENCE WAS A BEAUTIFUL CITY. Lola promised herself she would come back here to visit when she could enjoy it better. They were just turning the corner on their way back from the market when the call from Boris came. He'd had no luck on his end and was now as worried about Phyllis as they were. They told him they had a friend of the family coming at noon and that he might have some new information or ideas as to her whereabouts. They couldn't say it was Simon, for Boris probably knew he'd been dead for years. Boris said he'd call back around 1 p.m. as it was easier for him to call them. They hung up and made it back to the apartment. Simon hadn't arrived yet, but since they had nothing better to do, they started eating. At noon on the dot, Simon's door appeared, and he looked haggard.

"Dad, are you alright?" asked Lola as she raced to embrace him.

"Yes, love, I'm fine. It was just a bad night. I can tell I don't have much time now. My body is starting to fail in my own timeline. We *must* find Phyllis." He squeezed Lola a little longer.

"Did your Phyllis have any other ideas?" asked Jackson, trying to stay on task.

"No, none at all. How did you fare with Boris?" asked Simon as he joined them at the table for lunch.

"He hasn't seen or heard from her since she postponed their trip to Prague a few weeks ago. He made some calls and came up as empty as we did. He said he'd call back at 1 p.m. to see if you'd come up with anything," replied Lola.

"You told him I was here?" inquired Simon with a worried expression.

"No, we said you were a friend of the family."

"Right. Okay. We can't call the authorities because she hasn't been missing for twenty-four hours, and we can't prove she's here, or anywhere really because she didn't travel here by plane," mused Simon as he picked at his food.

"We haven't checked clinics and hospitals in America or here. She might have felt ill and gone to have it checked out," supplied Lola. She, too, was picking at her food. Jackson was the only one who seemed to have an appetite, and he dug in with relish.

"Good idea, though, unless she was near unconsciousness, she would have told one of us," Jackson said thoughtfully. "Lola, you go back to the house and check in with Marie. Then go to the library and call Phyllis' doctor. The number is inside the front cover of her day planner. Simon can call the main hospitals and clinics, and I'll go to the nearest emergency room here in case she was brought in by ambulance and didn't have any ID on her. I'll have my cell phone on for when Boris calls back or if either of you needs to get in touch with me. Let's meet back here by 3 p.m."

With a task firmly in their grasp, they finished their lunch, and each got to it. When Lola arrived at the house, Marie was in the kitchen and had spotted Lola's note on the counter. She asked if she'd seen Phyllis, and Marie said she hadn't seen her since yesterday at lunch. She was worried because none of them had been there for dinner and hadn't let her know. Jackson must have forgotten. Lola apologized and said she hadn't been able to locate her aunt since lunch either and asked if Marie had any ideas as to where she might be. The only thing Marie came up with was that the attorneys had called yesterday afternoon, and perhaps Lola should call them back.

Lola decided to start with the doctor and went to the library to call him. When that did not produce any results, she called the attorney. He said he'd be right over as he did not want to discuss things over the phone.

When he arrived, he had a large box with him and a grim look. Lola, sensing she knew the answer, asked what was in the box. Marie showed him to the library, offered to bring tea, and left them. Once she was gone, Edward set the box on the table and opened it to reveal the Archives. Lola and Simon had left the book in the schoolroom yesterday. How did it end up back at the attorney's office?

Lola gasped and said, "Does that mean Phyllis is dead?"

"No, the book did not simply appear this time. It was sent by courier," said the attorney calmly.

"Oh, thank God. But why would Phyllis send you the book by courier?" asked Lola, puzzled.

"I have no idea, but it can't be good. Can you tell me what's going on?" he asked.

Lola gave him the rundown and waited to see if he had any ideas.

"I believe there are both summoning and locator spells in the book. Only a Custodian can use them, however. As you are not yet of age, only an elder Evers could speak the words, and we seem to be out of elders," he replied apologetically.

"Well,......there is one," said Lola, biting her lip.

"Who?" inquired the attorney.

Lola looked at the floor, and in the barest of whispers, she replied, "My dad."

"Simon? How is that possible? He's been dead for years," the attorney said, confused.

"Yes, but he's found a way to travel here, to this time, but can only do it until my 16th birthday, so we need to hurry," replied Lola.

"We have a few days yet," Edward added.

"Yes, but we have a huge party planned for Saturday with tons of people coming," said Lola. "Oh my God, I'm forgetting Jane!" she cried out.

"Jane?" inquired the attorney.

"My best friend from Baltimore. She'll be arriving on the 4 p.m. bus," said Lola anxiously.

"I'll have a car and driver pick her up and bring her here. Marie can attend to her if you are otherwise occupied," supplied Edward matter-of-factly. He opened his planner and took note of it.

Just then, Marie knocked on the door and entered with the tea tray. She set it down, poured out two cups and gestured to the home-baked scones on the plate, and left them. They both sat and took a cup.

Lola took a sip and continued, "Wow, thanks. I need to be here when she arrives, but that helps a lot because Jackson is in Florence, and he can't travel back quite as quickly as I can."

"Is Jackson aware of the situation? Keys, doors, and the like?" asked Edward.

"Yes, he does now. My dad had a chat with him. We didn't know if he knew or not, but considering his role in the plot, as it were, we thought it best he be informed," said Lola.

The attorney seemed unaffected by this news and nodded his head before inquiring, "About Simon, can you get in touch with him?"

"Yes. Let me call Jackson. If I can't reach him, I'll go back to Florence to fetch my dad." Lola got up and called Jackson. He was still at the emergency room, so he wasn't with Simon. Lola apologized to the attorney and invited him to enjoy his tea while she went to get her dad.

"No worries, Lola. This is not a social call. You just do what you need to do," he said pleasantly. "I'll arrange for the car and driver while I wait."

Lola went up to the attic and opened a door. When she got to the apartment in Florence, Simon was pacing and wringing his hands.

"Any news?" he asked.

"Not exactly. But you need to come back with me right away. I'll explain when we get there," Lola said. Simon didn't ask and followed her back through the door. Within minutes they were in the library. Simon smiled warmly at the older gentleman and shook his hand enthusiastically. The attorney looked astonished to see Simon, who hadn't aged in the last thirteen years.

"It's good to see you, young man. I wish it was under better circumstances. And once this is done, I believe you'll have some explaining to do!" said the attorney.

"Yes, sir. I promise," replied Simon.

The attorney opened the book to the correct page. How he knew which one was beyond Lola, as she had been told that only Evers could see the writing. Maybe the attorneys had a special index just for them so they could guide new Custodians in their duties. Simon read it once and said he'd need some candles and one of Phyllis' personal effects. They rang for Marie to ask for eight white pillar candles, and Lola ran up to Phyllis' room to grab her dressing gown. She figured it might not be appropriate to use, but she was in a hurry.

When she got back to the library, Simon had lit and placed the candles in a circle in the middle of the room. The attorney was standing in a corner of the room, trying to look inconspicuous. Lola gave Simon the dressing gown, and he placed it within the circle. Then he took the book and spoke the summoning incantation, "Ea enim quae sunt amissa, venite inveniet eam et ducam eam in domum suam."

The candles seem to flicker from an invisible wind, but nothing else happened. Simon said the incantation again, and they waited breathlessly. Then there was a shimmer in the middle of the circle, and Phyllis appeared. At least, part of Phyllis appeared. She looked like a ghost or a hologram they could see right through.

"Phyllis! Can you hear us?" cried Simon. "Can you see us?"

"Yes! Simon, is that you? And Lola?" Phyllis whispered.

"Yes, Phyllis, where are you?" Simon asked, lowering his voice.

"I don't know exactly. It's dark and damp. It looks like the dungeons under the house, but I know I'm not in the house," said Phyllis urgently, looking about her.

"How did you get there?" asked Lola.

"I went to Florence for the afternoon, since I wanted to get Lola a gift from my favorite shop. As I was coming back through the side alley, a door appeared! I thought it was you, but I didn't recognize the man that came out. I don't know what happened next. Maybe I fainted, or maybe I got hit over the head, but I woke up here. I'm sorry I can't be more specific," said Phyllis, looking pained.

"It makes sense that it would be dark and damp. You're probably in someone's basement. Can you hear anything? Have you seen the man again? Are you alright?" asked Simon, clearly worried.

"Yes, I'm fine. And I can't hear or see a thing other than darkness," said Phyllis.

"Okay, Phyllis. We'll try the locator spell and try to find you that way. Just hang in there," said Simon as he flipped through the book. He looked up at Edward, bewildered.

The attorney approached, found the locator spell, and opened the page for Simon to read it. He said they needed a map and a pendulum. They grabbed one of the atlases from a shelf, opened it to Florence, and were wondering what to use for a pendulum when Lola unhooked the locket from around her neck. Simon grabbed it with a smile and dangled it over the map while speaking the incantation, "Quem quaeris illa honor credentibus: in quo ostendit nobis invenire eam."

The locket started spinning and soon hit a spot on the map. It confirmed she was in Florence. However, they soon realized they needed a more precise map. Lola told them to hold on a minute and ran up to her room to get her iPad. She opened Maps to downtown Florence and looked up expectantly. Both the attorney and Simon looked at her quizzically.

"What?! It's technology. We might as well use it," she said with a shrug.

Simon spoke the incantation again. When the locket hit the screen, Lola zoomed in on the map. They did this two more times until they got close enough to get a street address. Then they pondered what to do next. Sure, they had found Phyllis, but the existence of another person being able to open a door and the fact that she seemed to be their prisoner complicated matters. Lola suggested they send Jackson to simply knock on the door and pretend to be looking for someone. That way, he could at least see who lived there. Simon thought that was a good plan. The attorney said they could look up that information on the internet. But that would only give them the owner's name and number. The attorney said he might recognize the name and make further *discreet* inquiries. Simon gave him the house phone while he and Lola went back to get Jackson up to speed. Jackson shared with them that he wished his parents were there since they would know what to do. He agreed to go play tourist and see how that went.

He grabbed a map and got a cab to a few houses before the address Lola had given him. Then he took his most innocent American teenager look and knocked on the door. A huge man in a gray suit opened the door and asked what he wanted in rapid, fluent Italian. Though Jackson also spoke Italian, he put on a thick Southern drawl and asked to see a Vincente Azura. The man said no such person was there. Jackson got closer so he could peer inside and showed the man his map asking if this was not 3457 Via Del Quatro. The man responded that it was 3457 Via Del Gore. Ah! My mistake, Jackson had responded and thanked the man profusely as he backed down the stairs. Then he made a show of pointing the wrong way, and the man, with a chuckle now, pointed him in the other direction. Jackson walked to the end of the block and turned before hailing a cab and going back to the apartment.

CHAPTER 39
KIDNAPPED

MEANWHILE, back at the house, the attorney found out the name of the owner and tracked him down by phone to see if he was currently in residence.

The elderly couple who owned the brownstone was currently touring the south of France and had rented the apartment out through an agency. When the attorney explained about Phyllis, the couple were quick to provide the agency's name and said they would call ahead, so the agency complied as best they could. It turned out the agency had rented the house for the full month to a man traveling alone for work. Though the man paid cash, the agency still required all tenants to provide a valid credit card, cell phone number, and a copy of their passport. They could not provide this information without a warrant but were able to supply the attorney with his name and cell phone number. The attorney noted the information, thanked them, and hung up. The name brought no leads, and the cell phone was a disposable one. With a little digging, the only thing they could do was verify the whereabouts of the phone. The attorney had a man in IT who could track the phone. He called him and gave him the number. Five minutes later, the IT guy confirmed that the phone and its owner were currently at the same address.

When Jackson came back, he called Lola, who put him on speakerphone. He gave as accurate a description of the man as he could. He was tall, at least 6' 2", wide-chested, and had a strong muscular build. He wore expensive Italian clothes and shoes and spoke like a local. He had thinning brown hair and brown eyes, heavy stubble, and Jackson estimated the man to be close to fifty years of age. The description did not ring a bell for either Simon or the attorney. They hung up and told Jackson they would call him back soon.

They discussed the possibility of requesting Boris' help since, according to Phyllis, he had powerful connections all over Europe. However, the fact that this man had come through a door made the matter a little more tricky.

Neither the authorities nor strangers could be counted upon in this instance.

They decided to summon Phyllis again to check on her and see if there had been any developments. She was able to confirm the man spoke Italian in the house, though she only heard *his* voice, so he must be talking on the phone to someone. He had come down to see Phyllis and apologized for the accommodations. He brought her a chair to sit on and a blanket and said he'd be back soon with food. Once they'd spoken to Phyllis, they had a conference call with Jackson to discuss the situation.

"We need a SWAT team to keep track of him so we can burst in and save Phyllis when he goes out," said Lola.

"This isn't an action movie!" said Jackson from the phone.

"I'm sure Boris could handle it," quipped Lola.

"Just because he's a rich Russian doesn't mean he has ties with organized crime," Jackson responded.

"No, but if he has friends in high places, he might have access to specialized resources that won't ask too many questions," said Simon.

"True, but Boris himself would ask those questions," said the attorney.

"Maybe we could say she's been kidnapped due to her wealth, and we're waiting for a ransom note and have been told not to contact the authorities. I'm sure he'd go for that explanation," offered Lola.

"Also true, but what if this guy is using a door to come and go instead of the front door? How can we be sure we could rescue Phyllis undetected?" said Simon.

"Oh, right," agreed Lola, grabbing a scone from the plate, and taking a bite. A thought seemed to occur to her, and she added, "And what if he's got a bunch of relatives, who also have keys and join him at the house while he figures out what to do with Phyllis?"

"But isn't it a little extreme to kidnap someone just because they saw a person use a door?" said Jackson.

"Maybe he panicked. Maybe Phyllis fainted, and he didn't want to leave her in the street, so he brought her home, as it were," suggested Edward.

"But why put her in the cellar? He could have put her in a bedroom or even on the couch," said Simon.

"Then she might have run away and called the cops," suggested Lola. "Imagine if you opened a door and came face to face with someone. You'd want to make sure they kept their mouth shut about it. You might also think you'd get into trouble for letting the secret slip," she said as she got up and acted out the scenario.

"True. Jackson knows, and nothing bad has happened. And Simon traveled through time, and nothing bad has happened either," said the attorney.

"You mean nothing except Phyllis being kidnapped by another door hopper we didn't know existed," interjected Jackson.

"Right, you have a point. Edward, how many families have keys?"

According to the attorney, there were a handful of families across the world who had keys and could access doors much like the Evers. Most lived in mansions built between the 1500s and 1700s by an architect named Sandoval. He was a Freemason charged with concealing magical artifacts and other secrets. The keys were meant to lead back to a secret chamber where high-level Freemasons could meet in total secrecy and privacy. The exact location is known only by the original Freemasons and their descendants. That meant the first Mr. Evers was one of those masons and may or may not have passed down the Freemason knowledge along with the keys.

"Is there a list of current key owners somewhere?" asked Simon.

"My colleague in Munich says there is a spell to call an emergency council meeting. Whoever calls it chooses the location, though I believe wherever you are is the location by default. Only Custodians would appear, so I can't imagine there would be more than a dozen."

"You're saying dad could speak an incantation, and these people would disappear from where they are and appear here? Or would they stay where they are like Phyllis and join like a conference call?" queried Lola.

"I believe they will be transported here via a special door that will appear, and they will either receive instructions or they will feel compelled to enter the door. This is new to me too. Until an hour ago, I had no idea there were other keys. While you were out fetching your father, I telephoned my own father. He's very old, but he was able to provide a little more information. He was the one who suggested the attorneys in Munich."

"Okay, then perhaps we could do it in the dining room. We could ask Marie to prepare a light lunch buffet with tea, coffee, and cakes, then give her the rest of the day off. That way, she won't be surprised at the number of people here. I'm sure we can fend for ourselves for dinner later."

"Phyllis would be proud of you. Great plan. As soon as Marie's gone, I'll summon the others. Meanwhile, Jackson, are you okay to stay in Florence a while longer?" asked Simon.

"Yes, of course. Just let me know what to say to Boris when he calls back," replied Jackson.

"Tell him we've got a lead from one of Phyllis' friends, that you don't know what it is yet, but that you'll know more in a few hours. We may need his help if our Italian door hopper is a runaway or something," said Simon.

"Sure thing. I need to charge my phone now, so I'll hang up if you don't mind. Keep me posted," said Jackson.

Lola went to confer with Marie. She told her they were having some extra guests for a late lunch and that she could have the rest of the afternoon off. Marie said that was no problem and set out to prepare what would be needed, then got a lasagna out of the freezer so they'd have something to heat up at dinner time. Marie set things up on the sideboard and left the house.

The attorney suggested that he and Lola not be present in the room with Simon when he summoned the Custodians as the spell might not work. It was meant to be a secret meeting, after all. Lola agreed but didn't like to be left out of the loop. The attorney reminded her that her friend would be arriving at some point, and she'd need to entertain her away from the dining room for as long as this crisis was underway. She would miss out one way or another.

Simon and the attorney reviewed the spell to ensure they had everything they needed and that Simon would be safe. He was worried about languages since he only spoke Italian, French, and some German. Phyllis was the one who was good at languages. The attorney figured most would speak or understand English or be able to translate between one another. The most important thing to remember was that Simon should not mention he was currently dead or could travel through time. It might not be on the list of approved uses of the keys or be a temporary fluke so that Simon could instruct his daughter before she took over as Custodian. Later, after this was over, they could make discreet inquiries on the other artifacts and secrets mentioned by the Freemasons.

Lola and the attorney stepped out of the room and closed the double doors. Simon took a deep breath squared his shoulders, and spoke the incantation.

CHAPTER 40
COUNCIL

THERE WAS a ripple in the room, and the air seemed to move and shimmer though nothing else happened immediately. Then, one by one, ten doors appeared all over the room. The Custodians, some women, some men, wore identical shocked and apprehensive expressions. Some had been roused from sleep. The oldest was about ninety years old and walked with a cane, and the youngest was barely older than Lola. All Simon could say was *Welcome, Bienvenue, Willkommen, Benvenuti.* No one was talking to anyone else, but it was clear that Simon was the one who summoned them. He gestured for them to have a seat. Once no more doors appeared, and everyone had taken a seat, Simon cleared his throat and addressed the room full of strangers. Strangers who all shared a secret with him.

"Hello, and welcome," he began. "Does everyone understand English? Yes? Okay. My name is Simon Evers. I am the fifth generation of Evers living in this house. You are currently near Williamsburg, Virginia, in the United States of America. I, like you, have a key that opens doors all over the world. Until about two hours ago, I thought my family held the only keys. Until last night, I thought the keys were the only magic we held. This book, which we call the Archives, has so far provided three spells. I've called you here as my sister has been taken by an Italian man in Florence. She witnessed him exiting a door, fainted, and woke up alone in a cellar. The first spell let us summon her, or at least her astral projection, and she was able to tell us what had happened. The second spell enabled us to locate her. We do not know what to do to get her back. Obviously, the authorities are out of the question, and due to the hostile seeming circumstances of her capture and the fact we didn't know there were other travelers, our attorney made some inquiries that led to the third spell. This one summoned all current Custodians for an emergency council meeting. Who among you is from the Italian line of key holders? The man who took my sister speaks fluent Italian, and we can provide an accurate description of him as well as the address he is holding my sister." Simon was a little breathless as he looked at each face expectantly.

There was no answer at first. Simon described the man and the location of the apartment in Florence. Then he said he was sure the man simply panicked, thinking he would get in trouble if someone found out about his secret. Two of the Custodians exchanged a glance, and the older of the two spoke up.

"I believe you are referring to my nephew. I am from Rome, and my cousin over there, also Italian, lives in Spain. When Mateo, the previous Spanish Custodian, died without producing an heir, my cousin married his sister so the legacy could go on. Anyhow, I'm sure there are other families here who know one another. European countries are close together, and a few generations ago, it was essential to keep wealth and power within certain social circles. Families with keys tended to marry one another," said the Italian gentleman.

"Yes, that's very interesting, but is there anything you can do to get my sister back?" snapped Simon.

"I apologize, of course. That is the priority. If I may be permitted to travel to this address, I will speak to my nephew and return in a moment," the Italian suggested.

They all agreed and waited. The man took out his key, and a door appeared. He spoke the address out loud and was gone. While they waited, Simon invited his guests to partake in some refreshments from the sideboard. Once people had food and drinks, the tension seemed to drain from everyone, and they started introducing themselves. Other than the ones from Rome, Spain, and Virginia, there was a family from France, England, Russia, Japan, Australia, one from New York City, and another from Toronto, Canada.

Quite a few of them were shocked to discover they were not the only ones to hold keys and that their Archives held spells handed down from Freemasons. Simon had to ask the elderly lady from Russia what her last name was and when she said Ivanov, Simon burst out laughing. When she asked why that was funny, Simon apologized and asked if she was related to Boris Ivanov. Surprised, she answered that he was her son and heir and would take over as Custodian when she died. Simon was about to regale her with Phyllis and Boris' romance when a door appeared, and the Custodian from Rome came back. He said he had confirmed his nephew had the lady and that they would have come back with him but could not cross the threshold. It seems only the Custodians were allowed to appear in the dining room.

"I believe your sister will come home in the usual manner momentarily while I have sent my nephew home to be dealt with upon my arrival. You have the Donatelli Family's most humble apology for this unfortunate incident, and if there is anything we can do to make it up to you or your sister, please do not hesitate to ask. Otherwise, know that you may call on us at any time to claim a favor from any one of us or our descendants," he said gravely, hand over heart.

"I'm sure that won't be necessary. I'll just be happy to see my sister safely returned," Simon assured him.

At just that moment, he heard Phyllis knocking on the dining room door and calling his name, telling him she was home safe. He opened the door and let Phyllis, Lola, and the attorney into the room and introduced them to the group.

Simon thanked everyone for coming. They asked him to show them the spells in the book, and it was suggested that they should meet regularly to share information and get to know one another better. They agreed to meet again in six months, in Rome. Simon got a piece of paper and had everyone write down their contact information. The attorney would then share these with each of them. Alfredo Donatelli would summon them on December 15, at noon GMT. They all shook hands and took their leave. As soon as they were gone, he gave his sister a big hug and asked if she was alright.

"I'm fine, Simon. A bit of a scare, that's all. It was quite an adventure. I've just been briefed by Lola and the attorney. How extraordinary! I'm sure we both need our rest after such an ordeal. How about we have a family meeting tomorrow after lunch? I'm sure we can find something for Jane to do for an hour or so. Perhaps Jackson can take her shopping or something?" asked Phyllis. Then looking around, she added, "Where is Jackson?"

"Oh! The poor lad is waiting for news in Florence, and Boris is going out of his mind in Russia. I have to tell you about something I learned about Boris. Let's have a quick drink before you rest," said Simon excitedly.

"Alright, I'll have a bit of lunch and then run myself a long bath. Tell Jackson to let Boris know I'm home safe and tell him I'll call him after my bath," said Phyllis with a yawn.

Simon relayed the information to Jackson and suggested he take a commercial flight back home. Then he thanked the attorney profusely for his help, gave him a full account of his meeting, and sent him on his way. They would likely not meet again. Before heading up to the attic, he had a chat with Lola and told her about their family meeting the next day. He was going back to his own Phyllis and sleeping until noon!

CHAPTER 41
JANE

AFTER HER DAD LEFT, Lola had a bath and a nap. She was exhausted! She was picking up the dishes in the dining room when the doorbell rang. Jane! She dropped everything in the kitchen and ran to the front door to let her friend in. As soon as they clapped eyes on each other, the girls ran to hug each other, squealing and jumping up and down like schoolgirls. The driver deposited Jane's bag in the foyer and took his leave. Lola would have liked to give him a tip, but she had no money and honestly only thought of it after he'd already left. *Oh well.*

When he drove off, Jane was beside herself. She shared that her bus being on time and being picked up in a limousine by a chauffeur had impressed her no end. But seeing the mansion from the tree-studded lane, driving around the fountain, and being deposited at the front steps did her in. She was trying her best to act sophisticated, but she was ready to burst. Her jaw dropped when, a few moments later, Phyllis glided down the steps in a stunning teal chiffon dress that trailed behind her on the steps. Her regal posture, perfectly coiffed hair, and serene smile made her look like an angel princess—if such a thing even existed. Just before she made it to the last step, Jane asked Lola in a whisper if she was supposed to curtsey. Lola laughed and replied, "Of course not, silly."

"Jane! Welcome! It's so nice to finally meet Lola's best friend," Phyllis began.

"Thanks for having me. You have a beautiful home!" gushed Jane.

"Thank you, it's been in the Evers family for many generations now. Come, let me give you a quick tour before you go and freshen up for dinner," said Phyllis.

They went through a quick tour of the first floor, and then Jane was taken to her room, which was next to Lola's.

Jane clasped her hands over her mouth. "I get to stay here? Oh my God, I've never stayed anywhere this nice before! This is even nicer than our hotel at Disney World, and that one blew my socks off!" she exclaimed.

"I'm glad you like it. I'll let Lola show you her room, and I'll see you both at dinner," said Phyllis, on her way out, smiling as she heard the girls squealing in delight.

Jane dropped her things on the floor and plopped down on the bed with a contented sigh. "I may never leave. Do you think your aunt would mind if I moved in?" she asked.

"No, but your mom might," laughed Lola. "Do you want to chill out or see my room first?" she offered.

"Yours, of course!" was Jane's quick reply as she got up again.

"Brace yourself. It's completely over the top," warned Lola.

They ran giggling to Lola's room next door, and Jane skidded to a stop.

"Lola, are you sure you're not royalty?" she said in a hushed tone.

"No! I swear, though, that's how I felt when I got here. But there are no servants, so that's the first clue. There's Marie, the housekeeper. She comes in on weekdays to cook, clean, and do laundry. And Jackson acts as chauffeur, groundskeeper, and bookkeeper. Both those jobs used to be done by his parents, but they died in a house fire a few years ago," Lola said, recapping the information.

"That's so sad. I guess you would know how he feels."

"Yeah, we have a lot in common. More than you know, and more than I have time to tell you about before dinner. Come on, I'll give you the bedroom tour," said Lola as she pulled her friend along.

Jane was more impressed by the closet and clothes than by the computer and office stuff. Though she loved that Lola had a princess tower in her room. There wasn't much time left, so Jane went back to her room to get washed up and change for dinner. With a few minutes to spare, they made it to the dining room in time. Phyllis was in the kitchen getting things ready. They made teen chit-chat and decided to go sit on the front porch while they waited for Phyllis.

In addition to the lasagna warming in the oven, Phyllis decided to cook. About thirty minutes later, she told them dinner was ready in the dining room. Dinner was buffet style tonight, with three dishes to mix and match under the warming lights: Penne Arabiatta, mild and spicy Italian sausage cut into pieces and sautéed garlic vegetables. The dessert was a peach cobbler with vanilla ice cream.

The conversation at the dinner table was mostly around Jane and Lola's childhood in Baltimore. Phyllis thought it was an interesting insight into Lola's personality. Lola was much more animated when Jane was around, not quite so reserved.

After dinner, Phyllis excused herself, saying she was retiring early as she had had a very long day. She winked at Lola and left so the girls could spend some time catching up.

Lola gave Jane a tour of the second floor, and they decided to do their catching up with popcorn and a movie in the nursery. Lola told Jane about the general terms of her inheritance, her dad's letter, and of course, the new developments with Jackson. She obviously did not talk about the book, the keys, or the recent kidnapping. Nor did she mention the possibility of an arranged marriage. The first because she wasn't allowed to, and the second because it was just too crazy. She told Jane about the dance last week, about Phyllis introducing her to some suitable escorts for her upcoming social calendar. These suitable matches included Jackson and would also be adequate choices for dating.

Jane looked amused. "So, your aunt is your matchmaker?"

"I guess," replied Lola. "I don't know anyone, anyway. And even at our old school, there were never any boys I liked or that seemed to like me."

"There were plenty of boys who liked you. You just never noticed," teased Jane.

"I noticed. But they were jocks, really not my type," replied Lola.

"And this Jackson is? What kind of name is that?" asked Jane with a nudge.

"It's old. And we got off to a rocky start. He said his friends called him Jack but that I should call him Jackson. It sort of stuck." Lola smiled, remembering their first meeting. It now seemed months ago instead of a couple of weeks.

"I'm calling him Jack. See how he likes it. When do I get to meet him?" inquired Jane.

"He's away on business and should be back tomorrow afternoon," replied Lola.

"Business? How old is he? Forty-five?" Jane had a wicked grin on her face.

"No, he's nineteen, but he handles the things my aunt can't handle on her own. Like traveling to Florence in Italy," stated Lola.

"Oh boy! He sounds so sophisticated!" Jane said with a laugh.

They settled in for a night of chick flicks and gossip about boys, a topic Jane had a lot to say about, especially about Lola and Jack. She thought Lola should hold out for those other boys she might meet over the summer. And she stressed that kissing multiple boys did not make her a slut. Though she thought Lola was probably not the type to be interested in more than one boy at a time, so she shouldn't get too involved with one of them until she met them all. It seemed like good advice to Lola. And besides, Jackson was out of town, and she would spend most of her time with Jane so she wouldn't have too much time to miss Jackson. Because it was so late, and they were too lazy to make it back to their rooms, the girls slept in the bunk beds, just like they did at Jane's house. It was a fun night.

CHAPTER 42
CHILLING

FRIDAY MORNING, Marie whipped up a batch of waffles for the girls. They came down around 9 a.m., yawning and still sleepy. A few minutes later, Phyllis came in to let them know she was going to have a light breakfast in her room and may go back to bed. She would see them at lunch.

A few minutes later, the waffles, along with scrambled eggs and bacon, made it to the sideboard, and they dug in. The girls chatted excitedly as they ate, catching up on what was going on back home.

After breakfast, Lola gave Jane a tour of the grounds, and they decided to sit by the pool until lunchtime. Phyllis was looking better and seemed to be in good spirits. She reminded Lola that they had a short family meeting after lunch and asked Jane if she wouldn't mind entertaining herself for a little while. Jane said she didn't mind at all. She would wait for Lola at the pool and had a great romance novel she could read while she waited.

"Good, now that that's settled," said Phyllis, "let me take you through the schedule for the weekend. Tonight, we'll have dinner at the usual time. Jackson will join us. Tomorrow, guests for the garden party will begin to arrive at 4 p.m. I took the liberty to book the hairstylist and beautician for 1 p.m. They'll set up in the nursery, and we'll take turns having our hair, hands, and toes done. Won't that be fun?" exclaimed Phyllis.

"Wow, that sounds amazing!" beamed Lola.

Lola asked when Jackson was getting home. Phyllis said he'd gotten home early this morning and was resting. Lola asked Phyllis if he might give them a lift into town after the family meeting to show Jane around. Phyllis said he would probably be delighted to, and to simply let him know what time they would like to go. Lola then called him on his cell phone.

"Hi, Jackson! How was your flight back home?" asked Lola, and he filled her in on how he closed up the house in Florence, caught a cab, and had an uneventful flight home. "Jackson, do you think you could give us a lift to town this afternoon? I'd like to show Jane around. If you're not too busy, that is."

No, that's fine. I have a few errands to run, anyway. What time will you be ready to leave?

"How about three? Does that work?" asked Lola.

Sure, I'll meet you out front.

Lola and Jane raced back upstairs to clean up after themselves in the nursery. Then Lola walked with Jane to the pool and got her settled in. She told her the meeting with her aunt was about party planning and etiquette and that she would come back as soon as she could. Jane told her not to worry and do what she needed to do.

When the meeting was over, Lola was surprised to see Jackson by the pool with Jane, chatting away like old friends. As she neared the fenced-in area, Jackson looked up and gave her a huge smile. He got up and waved, and as his back was turned, Jane was miming something to the effect that Jackson was hot. Lola laughed and went in to join in.

"Have you guys been talking about me the whole time I was gone?" asked Lola jokingly as she plopped on a lounge chair next to Jane.

"Not at all," replied Jackson. "I was just getting to know your best friend," he said smoothly.

Jane burst out laughing and said, "Oh yeah, we were getting to know each other. But mostly, we were sizing each other up. I think we can agree that we both meet each other's *good friend* criteria."

Jackson lifted a shoulder in a non-committal way and got up. "I'll let you ladies enjoy your time together and meet you out front at 3 p.m. Text me if your plans change."

Lola smiled and thanked him as he left. The girls shared admiring glances as he walked back to the house. When he was a safe distance away, they started giggling and talking about him. They had a swim and swopped some more gossip. Then they dried off and went back to their rooms to get ready for a few hours of sightseeing and shopping in the great town of Possum.

It was so much fun hanging out with Jane. Lola had missed her. They made it back in time to shower and change for dinner. Jane got to chat a little longer and get to know Jackson a bit more. They had a tasty meal, and then the girls retired to the nursery again for movies and popcorn and asked Jackson if he wanted to join them. He seemed unsure, wanting them to enjoy their time together, but Jane insisted, saying they'd done the chick flick fest the night before and could certainly watch an action flick tonight. He accepted their invitation, and they had a great evening. When it was time for him to go, Lola said she'd walk him to the mudroom and winked at Jane as they left.

Once they got there, they shared a hug and a short kiss and promised to find time to catch up on the Florence situation as soon as they could.

CHAPTER 43
PARTY

THE NEXT MORNING WAS A BLUR, and all too soon, it was time to prepare for the party. Phyllis had her hair done first. Jane had a manicure, and Lola had a pedicure. After about forty-five minutes, they switched, then switched again after another forty-five minutes. That gave them plenty of time for makeup and wardrobe changes before the party. Lola had told Jane to bring her prom dress, as that would be a suitable look for the snazzy party.

When they came down, Jackson was already waiting for them, and he gave an appreciative whistle as they came into the sitting area off the dining room. He looked divine in a light gray suit with a Prussian blue shirt, open at the neck.

"Looking good, ladies. The men better have their game on if they want to get on your dance card!" said Jackson.

"What, there's going to be fancy dancing?" exclaimed Jane with a pained expression.

"No, silly, it's a garden party. Outside, with a BBQ and fireworks," answered Lola.

"So many things can happen under a starry sky! And you may yet be surprised when you go outside," said Jackson with a grin.

The girls laughed, and soon the guests started arriving. They had been so busy with their preparations that Lola hadn't noticed what was going on outside. The lawn outside the house was completely transformed. It looked like a fairytale! There were two huge tents set up with a canopy between them. Under the canopy, there was, indeed, a dance floor with a stage at the back where an orchestra was playing classical music. There were flowers everywhere, and Lola could see there were lights as well, though they were not currently lit.

Each canopy held two buffet tables on the outer edges, which were closed with clear panels to protect from possible rain, wind, or perhaps insects. They also held about twelve tables of eight people each. Lola made a quick calculation and realized they were expecting almost 200 people! She hoped she wouldn't have to dance with every single man in the room! Just off the side of the tents were smaller, circular, closed tents, four of them in total, which Jackson said were *powder rooms*. Lola couldn't wait to go check those out!

What was most astonishing, however, was that instead of the traditional white, or even the festive red, white, and blue reserved for the 4th of July, the color palette for the party was Lola's colors: lilac and pale gray. The very colors she was currently wearing, and that no one else was wearing so far, other than her aunt, who was wearing slightly darker versions of her palette.

They made a beautiful pair and looked very much like mother and daughter. Considering her father would miss this party, she was pleased to have Phyllis stand in as a parent for her. As much for the social aspect, as for the emotional one. As she looked beyond the tents, she saw posts had been planted on either side of the path in the woods to light the way when darkness fell. She could only assume similar posts would light the way along the path, so no one got lost.

Jane pointed out a few men discreetly hidden at various locations on the grounds. Lola asked Jackson about them and was told they were a hired security team. Some of the guests that were coming were high profile and would only attend if the security was tight. He also told them there were men at the front gate checking invitations. Guests then went through another small tent where a metal detector was set up, and bags were again discreetly searched. Looking over, Lola saw that tent opened onto a red carpet where guests were photographed, if they wanted, then served champagne before proceeding out into the backyard. Lola had seen this kind of thing only in movies, and she was wondering who these high-profile people were. Celebrities? Politicians? Who knew, but it was terribly exciting.

As Lola and Jane took in the sights and sounds, Phyllis was greeting guests as they arrived. She seemed to know every one of them personally, and each was greeted like a close personal friend with either a kiss on the cheek, a warm handshake, or even a quick hug. Phyllis hadn't insisted that Lola be there to greet the guests as she would later be presented to everyone, front and center. She had practiced her short welcoming speech about a thousand times. It was only a few lines, but Lola was sure she would muck it up somehow.

As people arrived and greeted one another, servers circulated with champagne and canapés. Lola didn't see a bar set up, so she assumed if people wanted something other than champagne, they could ask one of the waiters. She hailed one of them as he passed them and asked that she and Jane be brought apple cider instead as they were minors. He promised to be back in a moment, then headed into the house where Marie was supervising a team of hired caterers and wait staff.

As she turned to see him go, she saw movement in one of the upper windows. Someone was waving at her. Her dad! He was here! Lola excused herself from Jane and went into the house where she found him in his room. He placed his hands on her shoulders and turned her around.

"Don't you look marvelous! Let me look at you!" he said as he beamed at her. "I never thought I would see this day! Almost sixteen years old. I'm so sad I won't be able to dance the father-daughter dance with you tonight or even at the cotillion later in July."

"If you open the window, the music is loud enough that we can have our very own, private dance right here!" suggested Lola.

"What a splendid idea!" exclaimed Simon as he bent at the waist and held out his hand. "Mademoiselle, may I have the pleasure of this dance?"

Lola giggled, curtsied, and put her hand in his. And so, they danced, as though time stood still, for at least three musical pieces. It felt wonderful to be in his arms, safe and happy. Too soon, Simon said she should get back to the party but was hoping she'd come to see him before midnight, just in case he couldn't travel back here the next day. Lola asked about Phyllis, and he said they spent the morning together, and besides, he had another Phyllis waiting at home. He'd had enough time with his sister, not enough with his daughter. He was grateful for the extra time they had shared as a family these last few weeks; it made the transition easier on Lola. She gave him another big hug and promised to come back before midnight to see him off.

When she got back to the party, Jackson was introducing Jane to some of his friends. Almost everyone seemed to have arrived, and the level of noise and chatter was getting higher. She joined them, met a few she hadn't come across yet, and stayed with them until she heard the music stop and her aunt take the microphone to get everyone's attention.

Phyllis cleared her throat and said, "Good afternoon, Ladies and Gentlemen. It's so good of you to join us for this very special day. As you know, not only is it our Nation's Independence Day, but we are also celebrating two birthdays. My own, which in comparison seems very unimportant, and my niece, who is turning sixteen tomorrow. This is her first official social event—her coming out—if you will. Please join me in welcoming her to the stage."

There was clapping and sedate cheering from the adults and louder, rowdier cheering from the teenagers. It was only then that Lola noticed there didn't seem to be any children under thirteen at the party. Probably so that the parents could enjoy themselves while the children stayed home with sitters. Or, she wondered, was there a daycare tent she hadn't seen yet?

Jackson squeezed her, and Jane winked at her, and she made it to the stage without embarrassing herself. Her aunt greeted her with a kiss on the cheek and took her hand for support.

"Dear guests," Lola said and looked around nervously. "I am honored to be among you all tonight. Some I have met, others I have not yet had the pleasure, but I hope I will come to call you all friends before the night is over. As you know, I am new to the area, and thank you for your welcome. I'm very excited to be taking my place within society and look forward to crossing paths with you in the future."

Everyone cheered and clapped again, and Phyllis asked the waiters to go around with the champagne. A flute was delivered to Phyllis and Lola, so Lola gave her aunt a quizzical look, but Phyllis only nodded and smiled.

Phyllis called for attention once more. "To Lola Evers, may her beauty and kind heart be a joy to all who meet her! To your Health, Wealth, and Happiness!"

Everyone repeated "Health, Wealth, and Happiness" and had a drink. Lola took one too. This is delicious, she thought! She'd never had champagne. It must have shown because those that were closest to the stage chuckled at her expression.

"Thank you all," responded Lola. "May I propose a toast to Phyllis Evers, whose grace and elegance I hope to match one day. To your Health, Wealth, and Happiness!"

Again, everyone repeated "Health, Wealth, and Happiness" and had a drink.

"Dinner will be served around 7 p.m. Fireworks will begin after dark, followed by dessert. Please, enjoy the party!" said Phyllis.

And it was done! She was a member of society, they had wished her and her aunt a happy birthday, and now it was time to party!

She went back to Jackson, Jane, and the other group of teens. They all had champagne glasses and clinked glasses again. Jane asked where the birthday presents were, and Jackson said there weren't any as most people usually made donations in your honor to your favorite charity.

"What's my favorite charity?" asked Lola curiously.

"The Library, of course!" replied Jackson.

"What a wonderful idea. But I'll need to brush up on other ideas. I'm sure there are needy children and the like to support as well," suggested Lola.

"Don't worry, that's what these people do. They support charity and social programs. Just enjoy the party," Jackson assured her.

And a lovely party it was! The food was amazing, and the music changed throughout the night. At dinner, it was music from classic crooners like Sinatra and Bennett. During the fireworks, it was thundering classical pieces. When dessert was served, which was an adorable selection of almond-based, fruit-filled tarts, they heated things up with jive music from the 50s. That got the adults dancing, which eventually merged into disco, and even teens got the dance bug. Around 10 p.m., the orchestra took their leave and was replaced with a DJ, which some took as their cue to call it a night. Lola said farewell to her older guests and thanked them for coming. Then, she sneaked off to see her dad one last time.

CHAPTER 44
GOODBYE

SHE KNOCKED ON HIS DOOR, and when she got no answer, she opened it and poked her head around the door. "Dad?"

"I'm up here, love," came his reply.

She joined him in his studio, where he was packing up some portraits he had completed. The one of her was finally done and still on the easel, though it had been framed.

"I'm going to put these in the attic before I go so you can *find* them later as though I had done them years ago, and you only just found them. The portrait of you is a gift. I suggest you put it in your room or in the upper hall where fewer people can see it. I just had to sign it. I'm so proud of it and you, my darling," he said.

"Oh, Dad, it's beautiful," said Lola with tears in her eyes. "I can hardly believe it's me. I can't possibly be that regal and fierce-looking."

"You'll grow into yourself soon enough. Come sit for a while. I have a few things to discuss with you."

"That sounds ominous......"

"No, nothing ominous, but there are a few serious matters to discuss."

"Okay."

"You remember when we had our family meeting, I told you about the Custodians, the families, and our agreement to meet regularly?" asked Simon.

Lola nodded, and Simon continued.

"Well, obviously, I won't be able to keep up my end of the bargain. Also, some of them might do some digging and realize I've been dead for thirteen years. Phyllis met with Boris yesterday after I told her about his heritage. It's a shame they didn't find out sooner. But then I fear your mother might have perished sooner to get you to the house faster if Phyllis had left the house after I died. I guess it went according to plan," he said.

"It's irrelevant now. I just want to let you know that if Phyllis wants to leave to be with Boris, you might have to let her. And even encourage her to do it. I know it's a lot to ask as she's become like a mother to you, but she's sacrificed so much for us. She paid a price she never would have had to pay for the mistakes I made," he continued.

Lola was listening intently and nodding her head. They were seated at the little bistro table in his studio, holding hands over the table.

"*You* are the true Custodian. I've read the book cover to cover, and nowhere does it say you need to be eighteen years old. The only age references were you have to be thirteen to receive a key and use the door and sixteen to partake in Custodian training. I'm assuming because I was here and because we were within a month of your birthday, you were allowed to see the book and find out about things. But I'm afraid the book will come to you sometime tomorrow. If I remember correctly, you were born at 10:05 am. That should be the handoff. I'm hoping I can be there."

Lola's eyes were watering at the thought of her dad leaving her so soon. Her throat tightened, and she was unable to reply. Simon reached for a box of tissues and continued.

"Which leaves Phyllis free to be with Boris. Even without his sharing our legacy, she should be free to be with him, so long as she keeps her room in the mansion and visits regularly. But Boris will soon take over as Custodian, which means you'll be seeing him often, and the fact that he is privy to our ways means Phyllis can come and go as she likes with her key. Even if she married Boris, she could still see you every day. She would need to come here to travel anyway. Do you understand?" he asked as he searched her face.

Lola blew her nose loudly, nodding her head. She took a deep breath and replied, "Yes, of course, I want Phyllis to be happy and be with Boris if he's the one she loves. I mean, she's only forty-six. She's a got a whole life to live!"

"And how do you feel about becoming Custodian?" asked Simon seriously.

Lola squared her shoulders and lifted her chin. "I guess I'm as ready as I'll ever be." She grabbed hold of Simon's hand again and added, "What I'm not ready to do is let you go. It's been so great seeing you every day."

Lola started to cry. Simon got up and pulled her into a big hug. They stayed locked in their own little world for what seemed like hours.

Then, with a sigh, Simon released her and took a step back. "If you don't mind, I'd like to tuck you into bed tonight, seeing as I never got to do it when you were a kid. What do you say? Are you ready to call it a night?"

"Oh, I would love that! Just let me go say good night to Phyllis, Jane, and, well, Jackson," said Lola with a bit of a blush. "Give me twenty minutes. I'll be ready!" She gave him another quick hug and ran out the door.

She went down to look for Jane and found her chatting with Jackson on the porch.

"Hey, guys, sorry for disappearing like that. I was feeling a bit overwhelmed and needed a minute," she said, hoping that didn't sound too lame of an excuse. "Anyway, I'm really tired, and I think I'll say good night now." She looked at each of them expectantly and added, "Do you think we can have our party debriefing tomorrow at breakfast?" Both Jane and Jackson agreed. Everyone hugged goodnight, and Lola made for the library to say goodnight to her aunt.

"Dad's going to tuck me in before he leaves......" said Lola in her rush to leave the room.

"I understand, darling. Go be with your father, and we'll chat more tomorrow," said Phyllis, giving her a quick hug and a kiss on the forehead.

Lola raced up to her room, washed up, put on her pajamas, and jumped into bed like a kid waiting for storytime. She was feeling restless. It had been such a busy but wonderful day! She tried to read a few pages of her book but soon gave up as she was so distracted.

When a knock came on the door, she gave a start and yelled, "Come in!" She heard the door open and close and soon saw her dad's silhouette in the doorframe.

"May I come in?" he asked.

Lola waved him over and patted the space next to her on the bed.

"Tell me a story," she said to Simon as she rested her head on his shoulder. Simon took her hand and told her about his very first trip through the door and then about the mischief, he and Phyllis would get in when they were young. Lola laughed, and she would have liked to listen to him all night. But she was tired, and soon she fell asleep. Simon stayed for a while until he was sure she would not wake when he got up. He tucked her in, kissed the top of her head, and said goodbye to his daughter for the last time.

CHAPTER 45
GIFTS

WHEN LOLA WOKE UP, she immediately got up, grabbed her robe, put her slippers on, and ran down the stairs. It was past 10 a.m., but her aunt was still at the breakfast table, reading the local paper and sipping coffee. She had heard Lola's unladylike dash down the stairs and looked up as she entered the room. "Is there a fire in the house?" she asked with a smile.

Lola stopped just inside the door, caught her breath, and replied, "Is he gone?"

Phyllis' smile faded as she nodded. Yes, her father was gone. Phyllis strode to her niece and wrapped her in a warm hug, expecting tears. But Lola sighed, nuzzled in close, and said, "I figured as much, but hope springs eternal......"

They broke apart, and Lola went to get a cup of coffee and to fill her breakfast plate, and Phyllis went back to the table. As Lola sat down to join her, she noticed that all the birthday gifts and cards from yesterday's party were stacked on the dining room table.

"Are all of those for me?" Lola exclaimed as she mentally counted at least fifty brightly wrapped packages and as many envelopes. "I thought everyone was donating to my favorite charity?" she continued.

Phyllis smiled and replied, "You'll find most of the envelopes hold a card with the donation details. However, since this was also your coming-out party, a few guests will have thought a gift was more fun."

As Lola sipped her coffee, she walked around the table with a huge grin on her face. *This is better than Christmas,* she thought. She looked at Phyllis and said, "You realize there are more gifts here than I've gotten in my whole life!" Phyllis nodded and, when Lola simply continued to stare at the gifts, went back to reading the paper.

Lola's attention was caught by a serious-looking envelope that looked like it came from their attorney's office. *Wouldn't it be just like lawyers to send birthday wishes on office stationery*? She plucked it out and opened it. What she found inside was not a letter from their attorneys, nor was it birthday wishes. It was a letter of acceptance to a college Lola had never applied to or even knew about.

"Phyllis, did you apply to college for me?" she asked, holding out the thrice-folded letter.

"Don't be absurd, Lola. I would never do such a thing without consulting you first," replied Phyllis as she took the letter and started reading it. "Lola," she asked, "did you read the whole letter?"

Lola blushed and shook her head. "I got bored after the first paragraph," she admitted.

Dear Ms. Evers,

On behalf of The Academy, I am pleased to congratulate you on your acceptance for the fall 2020 semester. We are pleased to welcome you and feel that you will make a great addition to our student body.

As you are not yet of Custodial age and are next in line for Custodian duties, attendance in our two-week Summer Program, July 13 to 26, is ***mandatory****. We will expect you and your legal guardian on July 12 at 1 p.m. for Orientation. Simply take out your key and think—The Academy.*

Yours sincerely,

Ian Summers

Admissions - The Academy

Lola dropped into her chair and put her cup down. It sloshed a bit as her hands were shaking. She grabbed the letter from Phyllis' hands and read it herself, just in case this was all a joke.

At that moment, Jackson came in and exclaimed, "Happy birthday, ladies!" holding a bunch of flowers in each hand. When all he got in response were blank looks, he asked, "What's wrong?"

Lola slowly turned her head, blinked at the sight of him, and replied, "I'm going to Hogwarts."

The End

If you enjoyed this book, please consider leaving a review on
Amazon, Goodreads or Bookbub.
Reviews help me reach new readers.

Read The Academy, the next book in *The Evers Series*!

Join my Newsletter for writing updates, sales and giveaways!

ABOUT THE AUTHOR

Positive, uplifting books and stories.

Marie-Hélène Lebeault is the author of *The Evers Series, Clarity Castle, What Happens Next? Readers Decide Which Story Becomes a Book, the Blood Magick Trilogy, Holiday Shifters, Ghost Stories, Defenders of the Realm, Utopia, Chronicles of the Starborne Cadets*, as well as a series of picture books called Fairy Grandmother. She lives in Canada with her grown children.

www.mhlebeault.com

Follow on Social Media, she'd love to hear from you!

facebook.com/mhlebeaultauthor
x.com/mhlebeault
instagram.com/mhlebeault
amazon.com/author/mhlebeault
bookbub.com/authors/marie-helene-lebeault
goodreads.com/mhlebeault
linkedin.com/in/mhlebeault
tiktok.com/@mhlebeaultauthor

ALSO BY THE AUTHOR

Legends Reborn (Fairytale Retellings)

A Curse of Snow and Ash

A Curse of Thorns and Slumber

A Curse of Glass and Shadows

A Curse of Iron and Roses

A Curse of Briars and Hearts

The Chronicles of the Starborne Cadets

Stars Beyond Realms

Shadows of Orion

Echoes of the Void

The Nebula's Heart

The Starborne Paradox

Defenders of the Realm

A Journey to Power

The Quest for the Emerald Rattleback

A Summer of Discovery

The Quest for the Sacred Tree

A Summer of Opposites

The Quest for the Phantom Feather

A Summer of Courage

The Quest for the Kraken's Ink

A Summer of Destiny

The Quest for the Cursed Mirrors

A Summer of Unity

Defenders of the Realm - Special Edition Hardcover Set

The Evers Series

The Ancestors' Key

The Academy

The Time Walker

The World Jumper

5th Anniversary Edition Omnibus

The Traveler's Handbook

The Lost Key

Blood Magick Trilogy

The Blood Mage

Blood Magick

Blood Legacy

Extended Edition Omnibus

Standalones

Clarity Castle

What Happens Next?

Ghost Stories

Holiday Shifters

Echoes of Tomorrow

Utopia

Picture Books

Fairy Grandmother: Millie Goes to Antarctica

Fairy Grandmother: Millie Goes to the North Pole

Fairy Grandmother: Millie Goes to China

Fairy Grandmother: Millie Goes to Africa

(Also available in French, Spanish, German, and Italian)

www.ingramcontent.com/pod-product-compliance
Lightning Source LLC
Chambersburg PA
CBHW020320260626
47156CB00004B/1310

* 9 7 8 1 9 9 0 6 5 6 1 2 5 *